The Nine Days of Father Serra

The Nine Days of Father Serra

by

ISABELLE GIBSON ZIEGLER

LONGMANS, GREEN AND CO.

NEW YORK LONDON TORONTO

1951

LONGMANS, GREEN AND CO., INC.
55 FIFTH AVENUE, NEW YORK 3

LONGMANS, GREEN AND CO. LTD.
6 & 7 CLIFFORD STREET, LONDON W 1

LONGMANS, GREEN AND CO.
215 VICTORIA STREET, TORONTO 1

THE NINE DAYS OF FATHER SERRA

PUBLISHED SIMULTANEOUSLY IN THE DOMINION OF CANADA BY
LONGMANS, GREEN AND CO., TORONTO

FIRST EDITION

Printed in the United States of America

Author's Note

Sometimes a moment comes to a man of consequence which he can face with his life and say: "This matters, this makes sense. Out of all the meaningless chaos that sur-rounds me, this particular thing which I am doing at this particular moment has a past and a future, and there is a reason for my existence—a reason that men can examine, admire, hate, fear or love—but can never destroy."

Father Junípero Serra, a crippled Franciscan priest from the Island of Mallorca, was one of the fortunate men who looked at such a moment. This book is the story of the nine days that led directly to that moment in the year 1769 near the blue waters of the Pacific in southern California.

The Day Before

The Day Before

"K WASIYAI," THE priest muttered. He wiped the salt
spray from his face with his long brown sleeve and
pushed his battered spectacles into place for perhaps the
hundredth time that morning. "*Kwasiyai*," he repeated with
some hesitation, "is the weathermaker, is he not, boy?"

The Indian boy looked up from the log he was smoothing into a plank and shook his head.

"No, padre," he said. "You mistake again the weathermaker for the witch doctor. The word you cannot remember is *kwamyarp*. The kwamyarp summons the rains in the
winter and drives them away in the summer. It is he who
causes the sun to be born and to die each day."

Father Serra frowned while he traced the two Indian
words with his thumb in the sand. "I do not know why I
find your language so difficult," he said. "When I was of
your years, I learned Latin and Greek, French and Italian
with moderate facility. Now it is only with pain that I
learn ten strange words a day."

The boy smiled and laid aside his planing tools to run
his dark, slender fingers over the smooth boards.

"It is strange to me," he said, "that while the tongues
and mouths and teeth of all men are the same, the words
that come out of their mouths are different—even though

3

they speak of the same thing. Why are the words different, padre?"

"In the beginning," the priest explained, "there were only two people in the world. They and their children and their children's children spoke the same language. It was not until much later, when the race of man increased and spread itself far beyond the original home, that the words changed."

"Why did the words change?" the boy insisted.

"It is difficult to explain," the priest said as he turned his eyes toward the horizon, which was scarcely a line at all separating the sky from the sea. "It has to do with the change of climate. When men crossed the mountains and rivers and seas they found an infinite variety in the way the sun shone, the rains and snow fell, the winds blew. These things changed men's manner of speaking."

"There is another thing," the boy said thoughtfully. "The white man uses many words to explain what the Indian may say in a word."

"That is indeed true, boy," the priest agreed. "The more complex the civilization the more confused is its tongue."

"Civilization?" the boy asked.

"That is a word I cannot explain to you yet. It is enough for you to know that the civilized man worships the one true God . . ."

"And dresses like a woman?" the boy interrupted.

The priest looked down at the worn folds of his brown robe. "Only the priests clothe themselves—as you say—like a woman," he said, "but civilized men dress—as they speak

—in various manners. Some wear the uniforms of soldiers or the garb of peasants. Some men of certain elegance adorn themselves with velvet and satin and lace. But they cover their nakedness, boy, and that is the important thing!"

"These men of elegance I should like to see," the boy said.

"You will someday, to be sure. When the priests and soldiers and farmers have accomplished their work here, the men of elegance will follow."

"And I will be able to speak with them because I have learned their language."

"Far better than I have learned yours, boy," the priest said.

"Our language is small, padre, and before many deaths of the sun you will speak as I do."

"I should like to believe it. When a man approaches his sixtieth year, he should be finished with the new things that confuse and fatigue his brain. Yet, if I do not learn your language, what can I expect of the good priests who will follow me here?"

His sharp black eyes blinked from the effort of staring at the midday glitter, and his thin, bony face, deeply creased by age and quickly changing climates through the years, turned almost immediately to the Indian boy.

The boy smiled. "Perhaps it would be easier to teach the Indians your language, padre."

"I am certain," the priest said sternly, "that many a poor pagan soul suffers now in hell because the Christians in Mexico were too indolent to preach to him in a language he understood. No, boy, in New California the priests shall learn to speak the language of the Californians."

"If you say this, they will do it, for, like the Old Man of the Village, you are obeyed in all things." The boy looked at his Franciscan friend slyly. "I believe, too," he said, "that, like the kwamyarp, you can make fair weather and compel the sun to be born each day."

With a pained awkwardness caused by his crippled leg, Father Serra struggled to his feet. He shook the ocean sand from the skirt of his brown cassock and, removing his spectacles, looked toward the sun that stood almost directly above him.

"The sun, boy," he said softly, "is as old as the earth. It is not born each day."

"But my own eyes see the kwamyarp bring the sun out of the hills with his magic words," the boy insisted, "and each evening they watch him send it to die in the sea."

The priest shook his head. "Listen to me, boy," he said. "When the Old Man of the Village dies, you will be its chieftain. It is not good for you to allow your people to live their lives in error and darkness. I will show you—here in the sand—why the sun seems to be born anew each day."

Kneeling on the sand he traced a circle, which was the earth, and a larger one, which he called the sun. The boy's quick, intelligent eyes followed the priest's movements, while his mind struggled to understand the unfamiliar idea his friend was illustrating.

"The earth is round," Father Serra explained, "just as the sun is round, and it moves around the sun in this

manner. When our part of the earth faces the sun—like this
—it is daytime. As we leave the sun, the earth falls into
darkness. Each day the earth makes a complete circle on
its axis, which is at this point."

The boy examined the circles in silence. "I do not understand," he said finally. "If the earth is round and moves
constantly, why do I not fall from it? Why do I not slip
into the sea?"

"Because . . ." Father Serra hesitated a moment. He
did not want to take this time to explain the physical laws
of the universe, which, he was forced to admit, were not
too clear to him anyhow. "Because," he continued slowly,
"it is not God's will."

"I should like to believe your words," the boy said, "yet
I can see with my own eyes that the earth is large and that
the sun, no larger than my head, dies in the sea. I cannot
see the moving of the earth nor its roundness."

"There are more things you cannot see than there are
things you can see, boy. Here is a grain of sand. Let it
represent the things you are able to see. All the other sands
on the shore—this is what you cannot see."

"When I am chieftain, I will see and understand all,"
the boy boasted. "I will learn it from you, for you are wiser
even than the Old Man."

"What I know and understand may be represented by
perhaps six grains of sand, but these things I will teach
you," the priest promised.

The boy held out his arms as if to measure the coast
line and then stretched them toward the sky. "You know
this much," he said, "and you will teach me. You are wise

and you are good—like my own people. And you are strong."

The priest glanced down at his crippled leg as if it belied the boy's words.

"In spite of your poor leg you are strong," the boy continued, "for you are strong in your head and in your tongue. When you speak, your people obey. I have seen this. I do not understand this, for with my people the leader must be strongest in his arms and legs as well as in his head. But because you are all these things I have love for you in my heart and I wish to become as you are."

Moved by the Indian boy's words, Father Serra spoke gruffly: "Well, boy, we have wasted enough time on the sands with words and phrases. We must return now to the stockade."

The boy leaped to his feet. "And I have promised to help Manuel with the belfry today. When it is finished he will come with me to the coast and show me how to build a boat that will ride on the waves toward the sun when it dies."

"Poor Manuel. You should be helping him now. When you are not with him, the Indians laugh and say they do not understand his words and refuse to be of assistance to him. Instead I have been sitting here wasting my fine words as well as my fine art on you."

"We shall work all afternoon and perhaps we will finish the belfry. Then tomorrow we can hang the bell, padre?"

"The bell will not be hung until the last board of the church is in place," the priest replied. "Then we will hear its music and there will be a fiesta for everybody."

"The bell will be heard through all the villages across the hills and far out on the sea where the sun dies," the boy said. "I have told all the people of my village about it and they wait eagerly to hear it. I have told them it is the voice of the white man's god."

"In a manner of speaking it is the voice of God," the priest said, "but why did you tell your people this?"

"I thought about it for a long time, and I could see no other reason for placing an instrument of music at the top of the chapel where you often turn your eyes when you speak to your god. I told my people other things about the bell, padre," the boy continued.

"What did you tell them?"

"I have told them that when the bell speaks, it must be obeyed, or the white man's god will come riding out of the sea and destroy the land."

"That is ridiculous, boy," the priest said sharply. "Why did you tell them a false thing?"

"I do not know that it is false," the boy said. "It seems to me that such a thing might happen. Besides, my people were pleased with the story even while they were terrified, and the more pleased and terrified they were, the more stories I was compelled to tell them. I could not stop myself, padre!"

The priest sighed. "Well, go on to the stockade, boy. I do not wish to hear any more of your tales. If you were my son, I would punish you."

The boy looked at the priest with delight.

"How would you punish me, padre?"

"I would wash out your mouth with a piece of strong

soap. Now run. You need not wait for me. With this miserable leg I need much time to climb the hill."

With no more words the boy ran along the shore toward the path that led to the Spaniards' stockade at the top of the sand-colored hill.

Father Serra watched him until he disappeared behind the cliff. Strong and straight and resilient, the boy's figure was more like a man-made weapon, a spear, perhaps, than a human body, the Franciscan father told himself—and just as naked as a spear, he thought with a slight discomfort —naked as Adam in Paradise before the temptation and without the smallest shame for exposing himself in that manner.

The priest's thoughts turned to St. Francis as they always turned when he was alone. Such a lad St. Francis must have been before he learned that the soul was more important than the body. The holy saint would have loved this simple, gentle Indian boy, and probably would have concerned himself less than the priest with the boy's nakedness. As a matter of fact, Father Serra reminded himself, St. Francis was never far from nakedness himself. The holy fathers had commanded: "If you have two cloaks, give one of them to the poor," but Saint Francis always gave away both. . . . More important than any of these things, however, Father Serra chided himself, St. Francis would long ago have succeeded in conquering the boy's soul, freeing it for God. He, Father Junípero Serra, had found the boy's heart, but he had not been able to reach past it into his soul.

But there was time—in abundance. The priest breathed

deeply of the cool salty air and thanked God for giving him the time to convert the pagan souls of the San Diego Indians to belief in the one true God.

* * *

The military commander of the Sacred Expedition to Monterey, Gaspar de Portolá, had long been on the way to Monterey, where by order of the King of Spain he was to set up a military base. The Church would follow after, for it was King Charles's will that at strategic places between San Diego and Monterey military posts and permanent missions should be established to make secure Spain's claim to the incalculably rich and fertile lands of New California. Gaspar de Portolá had left Father Serra and a few soldiers and settlers at the post in San Diego while he traveled north by land to locate the port of Monterey, which had not been seen by white men since Vizcaino's visit one hundred fifty years before. . . . During his absence Father Serra might take as much time as he needed to establish God in the hearts of Indians everywhere. The Church would not repeat its Mexican history. In New California the Indians would be converted by love and patience, the priest felt, not by torture and bloodshed.

Before he started the difficult climb to the stockade Father Serra turned to look once more at the sea, wondering if it was the great body of water moving in an unchanging pattern of form and color that had charmed him into believing there would be no end to these long, wonderful days on the coast of New California.

He looked then at the single ship that lay secure in the deep broad harbor. The tropical sun poured waves of numb heat upon the ship's deck while the gentle-seeming blue waters of the Pacific washed against its sides. The morning mists that separated the ship from the land had vanished. . . .

Abruptly the priest turned toward the hill. The ship recalled to him that other ship—the *San Antonio* that had been sent back to Mexico for fresh supplies and a new crew of sailors. One of these days the *San Antonio* would sail into the port and then it would be time for the Franciscan father to move north toward new missions . . . but Father Serra had fallen in love with the very first settlement of New California and he had fallen in love with the people who lived there. Desperate though his need was for the supplies that would arrive on the *San Antonio,* he knew he would grieve when it sailed into the port.

Painfully he climbed the hill toward the stockade. The camp surgeon had warned him against this daily descent to the coast, but the priest, who had known the sea since his childhood on the Island of Mallorca, could resist it no more than the sea could resist beating against the shore. At a middle level he stopped to rest his leg. . . .

From the top of the hill nearest the sea a crude, rambling stockade built from bulrushes and pine boughs dominated its environs: the sea, the yellow cliffs, the squat hills, the valleys, and the forests. Two cannons faced the forests from a high wall of the stockade, indicating that the fears of the occupants were less of the sea than of the interior.

Inside the cleared area were other evidences of man's haste to protect himself from the perils of climate and other men. Long low tule huts serving as hospital and military camps filled three-quarters of the clearing. In the other quarter stood a building only partially completed but nevertheless giving an appearance of permanence. It was built not of rough boughs and perishable bulrushes but of carefully selected logs that had been hewn, then smoothed so they might be joined together to make solid walls and a roof. When finished this building would be the chapel.

On the other side of the hill and out of sight of the sea and the ship and the stockade, a village of about a hundred Indian families sprawled along a sluggish, perpetually shaded river. Farther back among the hills were other Indian villages, but on September 13 in 1769 this was Father Serra's port of San Diego: a ship, a stockade, an Indian village.

Behind the unfinished church the young Indian boy was already at work, following the commands of a friendly, deep-voiced Spanish settler who, once a carpenter in Spain and later a farmer in Lower California, now directed the building in the stockade. The Indian boy, speaking the Spanish he had learned from a Jesuit priest isolated for a short time in San Diego, was the single interpreter in the camp between the Spaniards and the Indians. His people had given him the name Boy-Whose-Feet-Are-Wings, for even among the Indians his movements were unbelievably swift, and now he obeyed Manuel Villalobos' directions with ease, repeating them in his own language for the benefit of his two young Indian helpers.

"Man-Who-Roars-Like-Mountain-Lion has promised to help me with my boat as soon as we have finished the small house for the bell," he said softly to his companions. "Let us work with more swiftness."

The other Indians did not reply but they worked as he directed them. They did not understand why Boy-Whose-Feet-Are-Wings desired a strange boat like the ones that had arrived with the great ship. He had his tule raft which served him well on the river, and surely he would not ride upon the waves of the sea where death lived. But in their eyes he was already their chieftain. If he carried logs and tule for Man-Who-Dresses-Like-Woman and Man-Who-Roars-Like-Mountain-Lion, they, too, wished to carry logs and tule.

When Father Serra finally reached the open gate of the stockade he stopped to wipe his spectacles dry again, for what he saw he did not believe. Instead of the usual mid-day lethargy that lay heavy over the camp, there was a noisy bustling he had not seen since the departure for the north of Gaspar de Portolá and his land forces.

"Amar a Dios!" he called out to the dozen convalescents from the sea plague who lay hot and tired and bored across improvised hospital beds, then hastened toward the main military camp, where from the gate he had observed confused activity.

Unfamiliar figures—men with heavy dark beards that covered their faces but who wore the familiar leather jackets and high mountain boots of Portolá's soldiers—were carrying water to a string of mules and three or four horses tied to the vertical posts of the stockade. Horses! There had been no horses in the stockade since Portolá's departure. As the priest approached the group, one of the men recognized him and shouted, "God greet you, Padre Junípero!"

These were Portolá's men, these were the Leather Jackets! Yet it was impossible. Portolá was surely in Monterey. One after the other, he recognized them, however, as they ran to greet him.

"The comandante has returned and would speak with you in his camp," one of the Leather Jackets said to him after receiving the priest's blessing.

Father Serra, hastily distributing his blessings, turned toward the comandante's camp. The men, their voices loud and eager, accompanied him, but he only half listened to their words. . . .

"We did not find the port of Monterey . . ."

"The maps were ill drawn . . . Even Costanso, the engineer, was unable to follow them . . ."

"We passed through a little Indian village not far from the coast in the midst of broad and fertile area. The comandante gave it the name of Los Angeles . . ."

"Farther to the north we saw the biggest trees in the world . . . red trees . . . they must be as old as the world itself . . ."

"Even farther north we looked down upon a great body of water. We called it the New Mediterranean. It looked to be an inland sea . . . "

These last words disappeared into the sounds of two loud voices which Father Serra could not distinguish, for they came from the far shore side of the area. One was the shrill, frantic voice of an Indian and the other was the heavy voice of a Spaniard. The priest turned to walk toward the angry sounds, then changed his mind. The trouble between Portolá's men and the Indians had apparently begun, but he had neither the time nor the strength to settle every dispute. His immediate need was to speak with the comandante.

The frantic voice now sounded terrified, however, and when the priest heard the Indian cry out "Padre Serra!" he turned back from the comandante's headquarters and hurried toward the shore side of the enclosure. This time he recognized the voice of a middle-aged Indian who on the following day was to be baptized as Tomás.

The Indian was struggling to free himself from a Spaniard who had seized him by his long black hair and was shouting oaths at him.

Father Serra recognized the Spaniard, too. He had known the fair-haired Miguel Viamonte in Mexico—a man whose calm blue eyes and warm smile and delicate features had betrayed the priest into believing that here was a man who walked well with God.

Now the priest marched indignantly upon him.

"Let the man go!" he commanded.

The Spaniard turned his unchanging blue eyes upon the priest, but he did not release the Indian.

"The damned savage was trying to steal my horse," he said.

The priest repeated his command and the struggling Indian found himself free of Viamonte's long white fingers.

When he turned as if to escape, Father Serra shook his head and told him to wait.

"Your Indians here are the same thieving rascals they are everywhere," Viamonte said. He had stopped shouting now and his voice was as soft as it might have been inside a church.

"Tomás was not stealing your horse," the priest protested. "I do not know what he was doing, but he wasn't stealing. Tomás is a Christian. Besides, he is not such a fool that he would try to steal your horse while you were watching him."

He looked at the bewildered Indian, who was trying to explain himself in his own language, a few Spanish words, and with expressive gestures.

The first time the priest had seen him the Indian was nursing a wounded deer, and he seldom appeared inside the stockade without an accompaniment of strangely assorted animals. Although the squat, coarse-featured Indian looked more like a camp cook than a child of nature, he lived as one of a great family of forest animals.

"Tomás," Father Serra finally said, "does not understand that the horse is a possession—like food and shelter, weapons and boots. You must remember he had never seen a horse before the white man's. To him the horse is undoubtedly just another animal of the forest."

"Then it is time for him to learn that it is not."

"You cannot teach him by beating him."

"I have found"—Viamonte's voice was still as soft as a woman's—"that it is the quickest way."

Father Serra looked sternly at the Spaniard's benign expression. "You speak only and always of force," he said. "Does it not sometimes turn your stomach?"

When Viamonte smiled he looked like a happy choirboy. He smiled now, looking down at the priest. "No, as a matter of fact it has no concern with my stomach. I merely want it understood that no Indian is to lay hand on my horse. I want it understood now."

Father Serra spoke to Tomás, but he did not try to explain the Spaniard's words. He told Tomás to go now and help the Indians but to stay away from the Spaniards.

Viamonte interrupted when he saw the Indian smile. "I asked you to tell him that he is not to touch my horse."

"I shall tell him in good time," the priest replied sharply. "Such a thing needs explaining. It needs an interpreter."

"I do not."

The tall Spaniard stepped toward the Indian and before the priest could interfere he lifted a heavily booted foot and kicked the Indian sharply, brutally, and with all his strength. When the Indian fell to the ground Viamonte kicked him again, then brought his foot down viciously on the man's face.

"The next time he sees my horse, he will remember the pain," he said, walking over to his horse and tying the rope the Indian had loosened. "That is the way to teach an Indian." He gently stroked the smooth neck of his horse and spoke again to Father Serra, who was helping Tomás to his feet. "You are a mule rider, Father Serra. You have no understanding of a man's pride in his horse." Then with no further look or word he walked arrogantly away.

Long ago Father Serra had learned to restrain the anger to which he was by his own violent nature quickly moved. This was not the time for anger, he told himself, but his hands were shaking as he stooped to help the Indian to his feet.

The arrogance and the brutality were not new to the priest. He had fought them throughout Mexico and he was prepared to fight them again. But the coldness was new. The coldness, the absence of impulsive anger. Viamonte wasn't even angry, he said to himself as he walked with Tomás across the area and left him in the carpenter's care. He did not act in anger but in contemptuous brutality. He could kill a man and never look back.

The priest was troubled, too, by his suspicions of what had brought a man like Viamonte to this new, uncertain land. For many years the Spaniard had been a slave trader in the West Indies and from there he had sailed to Mexico, where the fruits of the earlier and hardier colonists were ready for the harvest. Now perhaps he saw in the colonization of New California something quite beyond even his own conception of wealth. This was rich land and it belonged to nobody. The first to arrive with the protection of the Church and the Empire might help themselves without limit.

Hurrying to the comandante's camp he kept remembering Tomás's bewildered face and Viamonte's beatific one. Thinking of these things he almost forgot why he wished to speak with Gaspar de Portolá.

Once inside the camp, however, he was able to dismiss his disturbing thoughts.

"God greet you, comandante," he said to the man who rose to receive him and then knelt to receive his blessing.

"I salute you, Father Serra," the comandante said. "It is good to meet with you again in spite of the ill luck that has attached itself to our expedition from the beginning."

The comandante was a youngish, thick-bodied Catalan with the coarsened, weathered face of a man who had lived hard but well—a man who would bear inconveniences and hardships if he considered the prize a worthy and certain one. When he spoke, his eyes shifted quickly, then fixed themselves upon some object close at hand, telling his listener that his thoughts were concerned with something more important to him than the man he spoke with or the subject they were discussing.

Now as he talked with the priest, who without invitation had seated himself on a camp chair, his eyes and hands were busy with the papers and maps spread over his table.

"As the men have doubtless told you, padre, we were unable to find the port. I do not believe there is such a port."

"It seems incredible," Father Serra replied. "Vizcaino's maps were so detailed, so exact."

"He made them a hundred fifty years ago. In that time the port—if it ever existed—has surely vanished."

"Yet ports do not vanish. San Diego stands as it was described by the navigators of those same days. 'The fairest port of the South Pacific,'" he repeated softly to himself.

"And it would seem that the whole expedition must begin and end at San Diego," the comandante said.

"Begin and end? What do you mean?"

"My men are weary and hungry and disappointed, of course. I had hoped—I had even promised my soldiers— that when we returned to San Diego the *San Antonio* with supplies and additional crew would have reached the port. With fresh equipment I should have chanced a second expedition—this time by sea. But the *San Antonio* is doubtless lost, and if it is not lost it is perhaps suffering the fate of the *San Carlos*. The sea plague has killed more of our men than the sea itself or the arrows of the Indians."

Father Serra looked intently at the Spanish officer, who was still staring at the soiled, frayed map of the Pacific coast line. "What are your plans, comandante?" he asked.

"We shall return to Mexico tomorrow. For the time San Diego must be abandoned."

"You cannot mean those words, comandante. The Sacred Expedition has only begun."

"It has ended at the beginning, padre. I cannot ask my men to live on grass and roots and berries."

"The Indians live well on the fruits of the forest and the sea and the river," the priest insisted.

"Spaniards are not savages. They are accustomed to good meat and bread and now and then a bottle of brandy. Have you ever eaten bear meat, padre?"

"Yes, to be sure."

"For two weeks my men tasted nothing but bear meat— then for two more weeks they vomited bear meat. May God deprive me of my soul if I ever admit another piece of bear meat to the stomach He gave me!"

The priest smiled. "It is merely a question of custom,

comandante. You should have seen the consequences when one of my *gentiles* attempted to eat a handful of jerked beef."

"How has the work gone with the gentiles, padre? Surely the indefatigable Father Serra has converted every soul on the San Diego coast?"

"The work of the Church moves well. Though the very young and the very old still resist conversion, we have baptized many souls each day, and so far they have come to us. It has not yet been necessary for us to attempt to enter their villages."

The comandante picked up a quill pen and began to write as if he had forgotten his guest. "I regret," he said finally, "that your work here must cease, and yet I see no possibility of our continuing here. Our supplies, well extended, will last until our men reach Mexico—no longer."

"You have considered this well, comandante?" He felt that he had been dismissed, yet he made no move to rise from his chair. "This was a costly expedition," he continued. "Two ships—the one now in the harbor and the *San Antonio,* which will return at any hour with a duplication of supplies and men. The horses, the mule trains, the settlers' equipment and food—to say nothing of the property the settlers sacrificed at home to take part in this expedition."

"They gambled—as you and I did, padre."

"But," the priest said sternly, "it was not a gamble on the part of the King of Spain, who ordered the expedition."

Portolá jabbed his pen into the map he had been examining. "You always find the thorn that wounds the flesh," he said. "No, it was not a gamble on the part of the king."

"It is not as if the purpose of the expedition was merely to convert souls. It was the order of the king to claim for all time the right of Spain to this land. The Russians are reaching out already toward the northern coast. Military bases will follow their fur-trading posts. This entire rich coast will then belong not to Carlos Third of Spain but to Catherine the Great of Russia."

"We have discussed this many times, have we not, padre? Better than you, I realize the consequences of this . . . this failure."

"I wonder if you do," Father Serra said softly. He walked toward the table, picked up the pen, and pulling the map toward him he drew a circle around the name 'Monterey.' "Remember—a soldier of Spain fails only once."

A soldier of Spain fails only once. Gaspar de Portolá knew this. Yet he had not looked upon this as a failure but as a series of misfortunes. Storms at sea and scurvy were disasters beyond his control. The failure to find a port at Monterey was a misfortune beyond his control. What was he expected to do—sit on the coast and wait for the *San Antonio* until he and his men rotted like the fish that were washed to the shore with every wave of the sea? Already he was at work on his reports, which would surely prove that he was blameless. Until he had spoken with Father Serra he had not even questioned his blamelessness. He was sorry he had given the old man so much of his time. The priest never failed to disturb him, never failed to make him wonder if he had done enough.

He pushed his papers back and looked directly at the priest for the first time.

"We shall leave for Mexico tomorrow, padre," he said. "All of us."

Father Serra laid the pen on the table and turned to take his leave.

"I shall be unable to accompany you," he said.

The comandante pushed back his chair and strode toward the priest. "I think I did not understand what you said."

"I shall be unable to accompany you," Father Serra repeated. "If you insist upon giving up your responsibility, I insist upon holding to mine. I shall stay here with the Indians—live with them, teach them, and convert them to the One True God. Then I shall move northward and accomplish as much as I can in the time left to me."

For a moment Portolá could only stare as if he believed the man talking to him had lost his senses. It was like hearing that the Bishop of Mexico or even the King of Spain had just proposed to spend his life with the California Indians.

He cursed under his breath. If he had not been a formally religious man he would have cursed the Franciscan father. The stubborn old man! The comandante could not possibly return to Mexico without Father Serra. Even if he were willing to abandon him, he doubted if his men would leave New California without him. Father Serra was the most beloved Spaniard in Mexico—beloved not only in the Church but by the people—the rich, the poor, the officials, the peons. There was no person in Mexico who was not flattered if Father Serra accepted so much as a dinner invitation from him. Nor was there a man in the country so useful, and often so irritating, as the Franciscan padre to military and government officials.

"I can compel you to return," Portolá said angrily.

The priest smiled. "In irons? No, comandante, you cannot compel me to return. Let me explain this thing to you. For twenty years I worked on the Island of Mallorca toward this end: to teach and to convert the souls of the savages of the New World. For nearly twenty years I have worked in Mexico toward this same end. I shall not give it up to pamper the stomachs of soldiers. I am needed no longer in Mexico: I am needed here."

"You could not live a week in this savage country!"

"I can live as long as it is God's will for me to live. I believe it to be His will that I remain here. It is not for personal glory that I wish to teach the savages of New California. Personal glory I might have in Mexico. There I might sit and grow fat in a Franciscan monastery or spend my remaining years listening to the confessions of the powerful and the avaricious. But I believe that it is God's will that I share a dinner of herbs with the savages of this country."

"And when the Russians come down from the north or the British decide to establish Sir Francis Drake's claim to the coast?"

"I have never met a man I had to fight," Father Serra said simply.

The two men stood by the door of the camp in silence. Father Serra was a small, almost fragile man, and standing near the comandante his head did not reach the big man's shoulder. But Portolá was uncomfortable, feeling himself to be the lesser man. If he did not return to Mexico, only his wife would grieve. If Father Serra failed to return, it would cost the comandante his neck. Not being a man who hesitated to make decisions, he yielded.

"Since this is your will, padre, we shall wait a few days longer for the *San Antonio*."

"It will come at any hour. I have been praying for its arrival."

"Then take nine more days for your prayers, Padre Serra. Perhaps a novena will bring it into port."

"Nine days will surely bring it."

"Should it fail, you will return with me to Mexico—with no further discussion. You will make me this promise?"

Father Serra hesitated. Nine days. A novena. Did a man have the right to ask this of God? To ask that within a certain length of time—nine days—a favor must be granted. Yes, he believed that man, limited as he was in time and understanding, had that right—if the nine days were filled with work and prayer.

"I will make you this promise," he said. "If we do not see the *San Antonio* within nine days, I will return with you to Mexico."

The feeling that the days here would never come to an end vanished like the early morning fog. The priest limped across the clearing to the half-finished chapel to pray. . . . Later in the afternoon, when he felt the coolness that accompanied the setting of the sun, he walked down to the sea. Protected there by the yellow cliff walls he prayed again. If he had been St. Francis, God would have come to him and promised him the return of the *San Antonio*. But Father Serra was not a saint. He was only a man who prayed and God, for His own reasons, did not speak to him. He stayed on his knees all night, and when he got off them he was filled with the certainty that the *San Antonio* would return.

The First Day

The First Day

FATHER SERRA quickly wove the hours of the days and nights into a pattern that satisfied him. By day he worked, and at night he prayed for the success of his work. He slept during those hours in the middle of the day when the sun seemed to strike out at any moving creature, beating him into immediate submission, compelling him to seek a protective shadow somewhere.

The priest did not sleep easily. Sleep was not the blessed thing to him that it was to most men who lived in warm climates. It destroyed the continuity of his life, and such was his exuberance in living that he did not yield happily to unconsciousness. But even Father Serra respected the strength of the coastal sun, and during the hours of its maximum force he slept or rested in the shadows of the cliffs a few meters from the sea.

He slept close to the sea and at night he prayed close to the sea. He did not share the Indians' fear of it nor did he understand their preference for a tame river that changed only when the rains swelled it or the drought shrank it to a stream of moving mud and debris. Men who traveled across deserts and desert mountains dreamed rivers almost into existence—he had done that himself—but the water and the fertility and the abundance men dreamed about

31

actually existed here. Here it was the sea with its straight-drawn horizon that excited, then comforted him.

No one knew its perils better than Father Serra. In his thirty-sixth year he had sailed from the port of Cadiz to Vera Cruz to become a missionary priest. For ninety-nine days he experienced the dangers that accompanied all men who sailed the seas in the eighteenth century. He became familiar with hunger and then with thirst, the least bearable of all physical sufferings. The hunger did not disturb him, the thirst he bore with fortitude, explaining to his companions quite simply: "I have found a good remedy against thirst, and that is to eat nothing and to talk less." With the same indifference he met the dangers of storm and mutiny that made a nightmare of the voyage.

To Father Serra, twenty years after that voyage, the sea was not an enemy but a friend and one of God's chastising forces. If he had been a pagan in a land that did not know God he might have worshiped it as the chief god-source. Here in San Diego it served as his altar, and the familiar, changing tempo of the waves was his music.

Like the sea around the island of Mallorca, where he had lived until he was called to the New World, the Pacific of New California was not a sea of moods but one that followed a great yet simple pattern of color and movement. He understood such a sea just as he understood simple men who moved steadily toward a particular end. Men of devious manners and behavior he abhorred, for he did not understand them. He often wished men were as predictable as the sea.

It was not difficult for Father Serra to love and understand the Indians, for they were free from the complexities that rose out of white men's ambitions. This love disturbed him. It was invariably easier for him to love men who did not know the Lord Jesus Christ and often difficult to love those who knew Him and believed in Him.

This had been true first in Mexico, where he had found white men and women corrupted by unmerited power of life over other human beings. Out of this corruption had grown moral complexities that had no part in Father Serra's religion.

Bringing God to the Indians of New California, who had no god nor an image of one, Father Serra thought, must be like bringing God to the first children of the world when the world was young and fresh and beautiful. He would have to take great care. It would be so easy to give them the form of religion without giving them its essential truth. That had happened in Mexico. So eager were Cortés' priests, and many who came later, to convert the Indians that they had done little more than exchange a set of pagan rites for a ritual dictated by the Church. This, and the bloodshed that accompanied those conversions, must not happen in New California.

* * *

On this first morning Father Serra baptized three gentiles who were to leave the chapel bearing the names José, Diego, and Tomás in the place of the long Indian names neither he nor the other Spaniards could pronounce. It was Tomás, limping but undisturbed by his experience with Viamonte, who forced the priest to examine carefully his own methods of conversion.

He had already given the Indians instruction in the Catholic dogma, but this morning he wondered if they actually understood the meaning of the cross and the crown of thorns and the Son of God. When he questioned them, they replied in their own language which Boy-Whose-Feet-Are-Wings glibly translated for the priest. Even then he was not certain that the answers did not come from the quick-witted Indian boy who had long ago learned the shortened catechism by interpreting it for his people.

After the baptism and the brief Mass, Tomás seemed reluctant to leave the chapel. He stood at a short distance from the altar and stared at the baptismal font, the strange-smelling censer, and the five-branched candelabra in which a single short candle was burning. After a moment he approached the priest and gently touched the rosary that hung around the padre's neck.

"I am Tomás," he said, pointing to himself.

"Yes, you are now Tomás," the priest agreed.

The Indian touched Father Serra's battered spectacles and spoke to the boy.

"What does he wish to say?" the priest asked.

"He asks," the boy said, amused by the man's words, "if the jewel on the padre's nose might be given to him as a reward for the baptism."

Father Serra laughed and pushed the ill-fitting spectacles back into place.

"Tell Tomás that such a jewel is an adornment only for

the noses of old men," he said. "Tell him it is not suitable for him."

The Indians exchanged many words and finally the boy spoke again to the priest.

"Tomás believes he has seen as many settings of the sun as the Padre has. He feels himself to be very old," the boy explained. "He says that more than anything he desires the jewel for the nose."

"Explain to him then that when the great ship arrives I will give him the jewel I now wear. But until my new spectacles arrive, which I have requested from my friend Palou, I must keep these. Tell him for me that without them I would surely fall into the sea."

This time Tomás laughed and the priest looked at him in astonishment.

Boy-Whose-Feet-Are-Wings explained. Tomás had understood some of his words.

"Tomás learned a little Spanish," he said, "from the first priest who came here, but he has great shame of it, since he does not speak as well as I do."

"Tomás and I will speak Spanish together," the priest said. "Perhaps we can teach each other our own language in time. Explain to Tomás, boy, that since we both fall short of your intellectual gifts, we shall need more time."

He directed his next words to Tomás.

"Tomás, the chapel pleases you?"

"Oh, yes, the chapel is beautiful," Tomás replied.

"The altar, the altarcloth, the sacred vessels—all these things give you pleasure?"

"Yes," the Indian said, walking toward the altar again, holding his hands tightly behind him like a small boy who had been told not to touch the objects in front of him.

"Would you like to take care of these things for me, Tomás?" the priest continued.

"Take care?"

"Yes—polish the silver and gold, keep the cloths and the vestments clean and well pressed. Sweep and dust the floors and the furniture. Would you like to do this?"

"Yes."

Father Serra, who more often than not wished people into being better than they had the capacity for being, believed that he did wisely to select Tomás as his helper.

The Indian now wearing the blue cotton loincloth and tunic that the King of Spain had decreed should distinguish the convert from the savage, possessed an awesome attachment for the tangible objects that symbolized the True God and the Church. He could be relied upon to take care of them. In time, as his primitive awe diminished, a more genuine reverence would undoubtedly take its place.

Now as the priest saw before him the two Indian figures, the thick-set Tomás and the ascetically slender boy, it came to him that the Indians, too, had their Sancho Panzas, their Don Quixotes.

Tomás, who obviously served his stomach at every opportunity, was a seeker of comfort. When he rested after the midday meal he lay down on a thick covering of rabbitskin which he carried for that purpose. He was a man of things. He was the first to examine the small properties of the Church, the tools and utensils of the Spaniards.

Just as their physical bodies differed, the minds and spirits of the two Indians were violently opposed. The boy would never be moved by things. Father Serra knew this. If he ever succeeded in converting this boy, his success would come through an idea—an idea that would grow on the boy's imagination. The idea might take expression in objects, but objects would never lead to the idea. While Tomás was a man of things, the boy was a dreamer. But, unlike the dreamer Quixote, he did not dream of fighting windmills. He dreamed about the winds themselves and where they came from and why they came and where they went. In spite of their differences, however, the two Indians regarded each other affectionately. The Quixote loved the man of things even as Sancho Panza in his blundering way loved the dreamer and failed to understand the dream.

Then, while Father Serra guided Tomás about the sacristy, explaining the uses of the various vessels and warning him that certain ones could be touched by no one but a priest, he wondered how the Bishop of Mexico would look upon his methods of conversion. The good bishop would certainly question the dignity of a gift of a pair of spectacles in return for a man's soul. Yet what other course could a missionary father follow? He had the most precious thing in the world to offer, but before his gift would be accepted it must be interpreted through a desirable symbol —in the case of Tomás and many others, the symbol was personal adornment or perhaps an animal. The priest had learned this long ago, and although he had discussed it with his fellow brothers, he had never mentioned it to a bishop. Only a priest actually faced with the problem of uniting an Indian and a philosophical and moral system could possibly understand the difficulty. One might hand an Indian a pair of trousers and say "wear these," or an ear of corn and say "eat this." But to tell him to believe in an invisible God was a well of another depth.

Later in the morning Father Serra visited the sick of his camp, rejoicing over the news that all would now surely recover. Toward midday he returned to the chapel to speak with Manuel Villalobos, who was carving the letters IHS into a wide beam that was to support the belfry.

Of all the colonists who made up the expedition, the young carpenter, Manuel Villalobos, was the most heartening to Father Serra. Men of good will would make his work easier and more lasting in strange lands, but Manuel was one of only a few who carried such good will with them. For the most part the soldiers and the colonists were greedy, lustful, cruel, and at their best, indifferent.

Manuel was like the other colonists in that he did not doubt that the *San Antonio* was lost and that, the priest's novena notwithstanding, they would all return in a few days to Mexico. At first the failure of the expedition had angered the young workman and then it had saddened him. He was married to an Indian girl in Lower California, who expected him to send for her and their child as soon as he had settled somewhere in the fertile lands of the coast to the north. He had abandoned his worthless barren land in Lower California, certain that he would find up here the kind of land that gave fruit in abundance as a reward for a man's hard labor.

To Manuel Villalobos it seemed foolish to finish the
work on the chapel, for it would surely be destroyed upon
Father Serra's departure, but it pleased him to keep busy.
Early this morning he had helped the young Indian boy
prepare some wooden planks for a boat. The boy had
examined the rowboats of the *San Carlos* and had said he
must have such a boat which was superior in all ways to
his flimsy river raft. With such a boat he could go far upon
the sea. If he had time, Manuel thought, he would teach
the boy something about sails. The boy was eager and
patient. He was the kind of boy who, having started to
build a boat, would finish it. The boat would doubtless be
the only reminder to later arrivals that some Spaniards had
come before them.

Talking now with Father Serra, who knew nothing about
building but who took a childlike delight in watching its
progress by able hands, he stopped for a moment to watch
the tireless Indian boy. With the help of his two companions he was pulling a young tree up the hill to the
stockade with no more effort than he would have needed
for an armful of bulrushes. Manuel looked at Father Serra
and laughed. "They make me feel like an old man," he
said.

When the boys reached the open gate of the stockade,
they did not notice Gaspar de Portolá and the big, yellow-
haired colonist, Miguel Viamonte, who were discussing
the removal of the two cannons in preparation for the voyage home. At that moment a bough of the Indian boy's
tree swept across Viamonte's face, leaving a deep and
ragged scratch from his chin to his ear.

Angrily he turned on the Indian boy, who was still unaware of the two Spaniards inside the gate.

"You stupid, clumsy Indian!" Viamonte shouted.

In his surprise the boy dropped the log end of the tree. He stared at Viamonte for a moment, then picked up the tree and began to pull again, urging on his two companions.

Viamonte grabbed him by the shoulder, and he dropped the tree again.

"You brown-skinned naked cabrón!" the Spaniard said, "I'll give you a lesson in respect. When I have slapped your face, you will do me the favor of saying, 'I am sorry, señor.'"

Before he could bring the palm of his hand across the boy's cheek, the boy had seized his wrist and leaped behind him, twisting the huge arm into agonizing helplessness. When Viamonte struck backwards with his heavy boot, the boy released his arm, danced away, and laughed. Then he ran down the hill toward the river, leaving the tree in the middle of the courtyard.

The incident happened so quickly that Father Serra and Manuel did not even have time to walk across the stockade, but they heard the boy's laugh. It was not a friendly laugh.

"This Viamonte must have trouble even if he must invent it," Manuel complained.

"Viamonte is a sick man," Father Serra replied.

"Sick?" Manuel stared at the man of extraordinary stature. "He appears well enough."

"There are many Viamontes," Father Serra said. "They

are all sick men. And they have been coming to the New World for more than two hundred years. It was Cortés himself who said that the Spaniards suffered from a disease that only the sight of gold could cure. It is more than that. The Viamontes bring the disease of evil with them." Looking at Viamonte's face, gentle as it had been the day before, he trembled a little. Evil, he said to himself, has its own smell, its own form. It is as alive as the man who carries it.

Each day one of the converts brought a basket of fish for Father Serra's midday meal, knowing that in exchange he would receive the priest's daily ration of jerked beef—an exotic, appetizing delicacy for these people who lived on fish and rabbits. The basket of fish pleased Father Serra. Not because it was particularly savorous—it was not always fresh and it was never clean—but he remembered at such times that St. Francis had often paid for his lodging with a basket of fish, and the brief ceremonial exchange of fish for beef seemed to bring him closer not only to the Indians but to his beloved saint.

After his midday meal on this first day Father Serra walked down the hill to his private camp under the cliffs, lay down on his cloak spread over the sand, and slept for about an hour. He was awakened by the knowledge that people were staring at him.

Startled, he looked up and wondered if he was dreaming. His young Indian friend stood before him, naked as always, and huddled behind him, their faces tight with fear, were three girls.

Not until this minute had Father Serra seen the Indian women at San Diego, and his first thought was to thank God that they were decently covered. In fact, they were clothed with a modesty that should shame the ladies of the court in Mexico City. They wore skirts cut from soft deerskin and bodices of fibers woven together on a deerskin girdle, and only their legs and feet were uncovered. Looking at the girls, Father Serra felt shame for the boy. He might at least wear a loincloth when he was in the presence of women.

The three girls stared at the priest, one of them beginning to giggle hysterically. The others were quite solemn, but all three had retreated to some distance from the boy, poised like three sea gulls ready for flight.

The boy had not yet learned the habit of greeting or ways of using words as an approach to a thought that had nothing to do with the words. He said quite directly, "We want you to marry us, padre."

The priest was puzzled.

"Why do you want to be married by me, boy," he asked, "when you do not yet wish to be baptized into the True Church?"

"If you marry us, you will give my wives gifts made by the white man. They desire candles and a bit of the gold cloth you place on your altar and perhaps one of your bone needles. You will marry us?" he asked anxiously.

"You speak of wives," Father Serra said. "How many girls do you propose to marry?"

"Only three at this time," the boy said. "There are only three sisters in the family I wish to marry."

"If you want to be baptized and married in the Church," Father Serra explained, "you may marry only one of the girls."

"Then what of her two sisters? Who will be willing to marry them?" the boy asked.

"Each will marry one man, have her children by him, and cleave to him in sickness and in health until one of them shall die."

"Men do not live to be as old as the women. They face more dangers. There are many more women than men in our village. Surely it is not just for a man to have only one wife—especially for one who will be the chieftain. I have need of many men-children."

"In the sight of the One True God," the priest said sternly, "you may have only one wife, boy. If you wish to marry three women, you will have to be married by your medicine man."

"I do not desire this. The medicine man is without strength and courage. I do not admire him. Too, I have already promised the girls your gifts. Now I do not know what is best to do. I shall have to think for several settings of the sun about what you have said."

"I will pray to God for the salvation of your soul, boy," Father Serra replied.

"If you baptize us, you will give us new names—names like your own, will you not?" the boy asked.

"Yes."

"Then I wish you to give me your name. You are the greatest among the white men."

"You want my name—Junípero?" the priest asked.

"What is this junípero which is your name?"

"It is a tree that grows in the forest."

"You are a tree that grows in the forest?"

"Junípero," the priest explained, "was the name of a humble companion of St. Francis. St. Francis was the father of us all and Junípero was the most modest of his disciples. So modest was he and without vanity that St. Francis once said: 'Junípero, Junípero, would that God would send me a whole grove of juníperos!'"

"St. Francis was the greatest one?"

"He was the greatest among the saints."

"Then I shall take his name. I am the most intelligent and the strongest of the Indians. It is perhaps best that I should have the name of this St. Francis, is it not true?"

Father Serra smiled. "I must say that the name of the humble Junípero is hardly appropriate for you. However, it is agreed that when you are baptized you shall have the name of Francisco. But not San Francisco. You are not a saint nor are you likely to achieve sainthood in this lifetime."

"And my wives—my wife, if I must content myself with one—will have a Spanish name?"

"When she is baptized, yes."

"She will have candles and a bit of the altarcloth?"

"She and her sisters, too, may have candles and they shall have material like the altarcloth," Father Serra said.

The boy spoke then to the girls in his own language, explaining what the priest had promised, then telling them to go back to the river not by climbing the hill but by walking the long way around it past the cliff. Two of the girls did not hesitate and were quickly out of sight behind the cliff. The third one waited.

Father Serra looked at her shyly as he always looked at women. For him there were only two kinds of women: good and bad, but in the eyes of other men this one would be lovely, he told himself; this would be the one the boy would wish, of course, to marry. Taller than Father Serra, she was several inches shorter than the boy, but she had his slimness, his gold-brown skin, his straight black hair. Her hair was longer than the boy's and she kept it from falling across her face by tying it back with a wide band of doeskin. She had a wide and beautiful mouth and deep black eyes much like the boy's except for a wider space between them.

She spoke softly to the boy, moving between him and Father Serra and placing her hand on his shoulder. There was something womanly about the gesture, Father Serra thought—as if she were trying to protect him from someone.

The boy laughed and again told her to return to the river. She moved away slowly, looking back several times. When she reached the cliff she turned again and smiled. Father Serra sat for a moment without saying anything. Such a smile was the power of women over men, he said to himself. In such a manner the first woman of the world must have smiled.

"She feared to leave me," the boy was saying. "She fears that harm might come to me. I had to explain that no harm could come to me—I am the strongest and the fleetest of foot. I am Francisco."

"It is evident to me that I must tell you more of Francisco, to whom strength of body and fleetness of foot were not the most important things," Father Serra said.

"I wish to know everything of the great man who bore my name."

Father Serra carried in his mind hundreds of stories of St. Francis and the other saints. What should he tell this boy? That as a young man St. Francis had wealth and beautiful clothes and fine foods, but taking the vow of poverty, he had given everything to the poor? This would have no meaning for the Indian boy. The Indians had few possessions, but they had the same possessions. He might tell him about St. Francis, who ate from a dish with a leper whom he believed he had offended. Leprosy was another thing the boy would not understand. His people died in combat with forces of nature stronger than they or, he supposed, they sometimes died of malnutrition, but not from diseases.

From where he was sitting the priest could see a mass of pinkish rocks that seemed to grow out of the ocean not far from the shore. Covered with sea marigolds, the rocks at a distance looked less like rocks than a treasure of gold that had suddenly risen from the ocean bed. They served, too, as a point of departure for hundreds of web-footed pelicans who were catching fish in their grotesque pouches from the shallow waters. Watching the pelicans, Father Serra spoke to the boy who sat wordlessly at his side.

"St. Francis," he said, "was a friend of all the animals of

the forest. Even the smallest of the birds loved him, and when he spoke to them they understood what he said."

"What words did he speak?" the boy asked.

"One morning when he saw many birds resting in a group of trees, he stopped to speak to them, saying, 'My brothers, God give you peace. You should praise your Creator always: Him who has given you feathers for clothing, wings for flight, and all that you have need of. God has made you noble among His creatures, for He has given you a dwelling high in the air, and though you neither sow nor reap, He yet protects you and governs you without any care of your own.'"

"They listened to his words?"

"They spread out their wings in contentment and listened and showed no fear of him, even though he moved among them. Only when he had blessed them with the sign of the cross and bade them depart did they fly away."

The boy understood only a few of the priest's words, but his meaning was clear. When he had thought about it for a moment he asked, "What of the other animals? He was their friend, too?"

"He tamed the wildest wolf of the mountains," Father Serra continued, "and he was a friend to the poorest worm. The worms and insects he picked up from the road where they might be crushed and set them down in safety. All life—even that of plants and trees—was sacred to him, because it came from God."

"I do not understand how he did this. When I approach the sea birds, they fly in fear."

"There are many things you will not understand, boy.

until you understand the love of God, and of His Son who was greater even than St. Francis."

"There was a greater one? One stronger and braver and handsomer?"

"Yes—and other things of more importance."

"Then I must . . ."

Father Serra followed the boy's thinking and replied with some sternness, "No, you may not have His name. You shall have the name of Francisco. But let us speak of other things. What of your own wedding gift, boy? You spoke only of my gifts to your bride."

"I have need of nothing," the boy said.

"You would perhaps like my mule? He is too old and tired to make the trip on the ship."

"Your mule? You wish to give me your mule?" He smiled. It was the smile, the priest told himself sadly, of a man who had been offered not a mule but the Kingdom of Heaven. "I should like to have the mule." He looked at the priest and spoke eagerly. "I will work in the stockade for the mule. When you think I have worked enough days for the mule, you will give him to me."

"You can work in the stockade for other things—for tools and seeds—but a man does not work for a wedding gift. A man gives another man a wedding gift because he loves him and wants him to have it."

The boy got to his feet and walked slowly away. Father Serra wondered if he had offended him. Then he lay down to sleep again.

When he woke up the boy was sitting beside him once more. "I have love in my heart for you, padre," the boy said. "I wish to make you a gift. When it is finished, I will give you my boat."

The boy has a great heart and a complete innocence, Father Serra said to himself. When he knows God he will surely be worthy of his baptismal name.

"There will be no room on the ship for another boat," he said, "so this gift I may not accept from you. Make me another gift, boy, with your own hands—one I may always carry with me."

The boy thought for a long time. "I know now," he said finally. "I will make this thing and bring it to you. I go to do it now. I, Francisco." He ran up the hill to the stockade and down the other side to the river. This was the shortest way—the one he had forbidden to the girls.

By leaning heavily upon his stick and stopping frequently to rest, Father Serra climbed the hill to his own camp and began work on the adaptation of the church ritual to services the Indian converts of New California would understand.

He was not without experience. For nine years he had worked among the Indians of the Pamé Nation in northern Mexico. There he had learned that one vivid pageant in which the Indians played the major roles was worth more than a hundred sermons, that one service in the local dialect had more value than a hundred spoken and sung in Latin.

In Mexico the equipment for pageantry was available and he had taught the Indians how, in dramatic, realistic form, to present the Birth of Christ, the Crucifixion, the

Descent from the Cross, the Holy Burial, the Procession of
the Risen Lord, and the Ceremony of the Washing of the
Disciples' Feet. If, in their playful naïveté, they did many
things that would have offended the bishops of Mexico
City and Madrid and Rome, they did not offend Father
Serra. There was a sincerity about their crude performance
that delighted him.

At San Diego Father Serra was handicapped by the lack
of properties. Even his supply of candles had been exhausted, and he could only hope that an abundant supply
would arrive by the *San Antonio*. In the long letters he had
sent back to Mexico by the captain of the ship he had
begged for many things, and heading the lists of his re-
quests were, first, candles and, second, church bells. Only
the priests who had worked with the Indians understood
the importance of candles and bells.

He was handicapped, too, by his slowness in learning the
Indian languages. He had no ear for dialects and learned
them only after long, painstaking study. It disturbed him—
just as it had disturbed him years before to discover that
he had no ear for music, that when he sang—and he loved
to sing—the melody was quite unlike anything that had
ever been heard.

Father Serra would try to crowd into the next eight days
what he had accomplished among the Pamé Indians in nine
years. Tomorrow, he decided, he would pay his first visit
to their village.

He had been working for more than two hours when one
of Portolá's young corporals appeared in his doorway and

told him that the comandante wished to speak with him—that he would have the kindness to come immediately to his headquarters.

Father Serra rose to his feet, then reconsidered Portolá's request, and sat down again.

"Tell the comandante," he said, "that I shall be at his disposal during the next half hour. I shall be at his disposal here."

A few minutes later Gaspar de Portolá and Miguel Viamonte walked into his camp. Without his usual courteous greeting, the comandante began to speak.

"I have been giving my attention to the problems of discipline in this country, Father Serra," he said pompously, "and it has been brought to my attention that during my absence a false impression has been given as to the position here of the white man."

"I do not understand you, comandante."

"For example, your Indian boy was rude and clumsy and behaved outrageously to one of our colonists. I hope you have explained to him since that white men are masters here."

"When I spoke with the boy later, I am afraid we talked for the most part about his immortal soul. I find it monstrous for a group of white men to come into the land of another people and announce that we are masters. I think it would be a little more becoming of us to come as visitors —with the hope that we would be acceptable to our hosts."

"You forget that you are dealing with savages," Viamonte interrupted.

"You find these people savages?" the priest said. "I find them friendly and helpful."

"The Indian boy conducted himself this morning like a savage," Viamonte said.

"Yet his behavior was less savage than yours yesterday when you brutalized a defenseless Indian," Father Serra said sternly. "Nevertheless, I shall reprove him. These are naïve people. They have not yet learned the white man's custom, which is to strike a man and tell him to say he is sorry."

"The white man's customs have proved their effectiveness in all parts of the world," Viamonte said. "Why change them?"

The priest sighed. "I suspect that you are moved less by the boy's rudeness than by his agility. I watched the scene this morning. The beautiful agility of youth. I envy it, too." He rose from his chair and moved toward the door as if to dismiss his visitors.

"I find this all ridiculous," he added. "I find you, Señor Viamonte, behaving like a boy who has been beaten by another and runs to tell his father."

When Viamonte merely smiled, Father Serra regretted his words. The Spaniard was moved again, he knew, to that calculating and terrifying anger.

The comandante, who seldom listened while others spoke, again took hold of the conversation.

"I shall take no action against your Indian boy now," he said, "but I shall depend upon you to see that he does not conduct himself in such a manner again. But there is another thing of which I wish to speak. I saw three girls from the village walking around the hill to the river. Some of my soldiers saw them, too."

"Yes. I hope to bring them into the Church."

"You do not propose to bring them to the chapel in the stockade?"

"Certainly. Why not?"

Portolá sighed. "For many months my soldiers have seen no women. The sight of them now makes them . . . restless. It was observed that one of the girls was beautiful."

"The object of our expedition," the priest said, "is to convert the Indians and to establish friendly relations between our settlers and the natives. This is not an invasion, comandante, and there can be none of the excesses that accompany invasions."

"My men are not saints," Portolá said. "Wherever they have gone they have found women to satisfy their lusts. You know this."

"I know that in New California the Indian women are to be treated like women everywhere. I shall not oppose marriage, but I shall oppose violent, adulterous behavior."

"I oppose it too, padre. For that reason I wish the women of the village to be kept out of the stockade. Within a short time we shall be gone from here. In the meantime, let us keep the women in their village and out of sight of the men. Even now it may be too late. Even now the men may decide to make a visit to the village."

Father Serra was persistent. "When we leave for the north after the arrival of the *San Antonio* we propose to leave some colonists and a few soldiers here, comandante. Is it not important to establish the pattern of behavior it is their obligation to follow?"

Portolá moved toward the door. "I find you very difficult, padre. Your premise is that a man is a saint. I know that he is not. I can only keep temptation from him."

Portolá walked through the doorway, but Viamonte hesitated for a moment before he followed.

"I will make no promises about my personal conduct, since that does not concern you. I will, however, make you this promise. The next time there is trouble between a white man and an Indian, there will not be time for a confession to the holy father."

When the priest made no reply, Viamonte continued: "The comandante erred in trying to explain to you the position of the white man. It is something a mule rider could not understand."

With a great effort Father Serra spoke without anger. "Once before you spoke of my mule. I have no shame for my mule nor for any humble animal that walks on the earth. There can be no shame in humility."

"Then when the comandante deliberately selected the most miserable mule in Mexico for you to ride to California you were doubtless grateful to him. I should not have been. I should have spit in his face."

When the voices of the two men had completely vanished, Father Serra had already plunged into his unfinished work. For a minute he had considered Viamonte's words. It was no doubt true that Portolá had selected for him the mule most likely to collapse on the long journey. It was a petty, a malicious thing to do, but the comandante was a man of small moral stature, he knew. It was perhaps a series of such pettinesses that had come between him and the discovery of the port of Monterey. Smallness and vision never shared the same soul. He would pray for growth in the comandante's vision.

The Second Day

The Second Day

THE SEA, so sharp and black during the night, had softened to a gray monotony unbroken even by a horizon, for the early-morning mists blended sea and sky and land into a mysterious whole, and even the anchored ship was not an inanimate object but a grayish mass without form or substance. Except for the waves that came in white and with a muted violence, the earth seemed to be turning in gray silence.

It was a pity to disturb such quiet, Father Serra thought while he prepared to climb the hill, by so much as walking through the grass or pushing aside the small branches of the scrub oaks that covered the hillside. The earth lay in silence as if after licking its wounds it had fallen deep asleep to let them heal. A pity to open them up again, yet as surely as the earth must awaken each day the wounds must open and new ones be inflicted. For a short time the earth was secure against its enemies. The small fish were safe from the hawks, the rabbits from the mountain eagles. The squirrels could conceal themselves from the martens, and the white-tailed does and their fawns from the bears and wildcats. Men were protected by sleep from other men.

The priest, holding close around his body the folds of his

long gown, climbed the hill today with less pain to his leg than usual. The daily sea baths were apparently taking away its soreness, and the thought alarmed him a little. For twenty years his leg had given him a great deal of trouble; for twenty years it had also served as a reminder to him of his ancient weakness, which he had never completely conquered but had kept well in control. That weakness was his vanity.

From the time he was seventeen years old and had become more familiar with the lives of the saints than with those of his own family he had directed his life to follow that of St. Francis, and out of this direction had grown his vanity. So vigorously did he apply the rules of St. Francis' life to his own that he had come almost to identify himself with his beloved saint. He had seen the danger in it and for that reason had given himself the name of the least pretentious of all the Franciscans—Juniper, the jester. But in spite of the name he had striven toward the sainthood that the founder of the Franciscan Order had reached, always falling short, he had ultimately to confess, as a man is always doomed to fall short of sainthood.

The trouble with his leg had come from an effort in his later years to identify himself once more with the saint. When he had reached the port of the New World he was determined to walk from Vera Cruz to Mexico City—a hard week's journey on foot through uncleared forests along a rocky, muddy road that lay for short distances in valleys, then rose to heights of ten thousand feet. St. Francis, he had told himself, would have scorned to make

the journey on muleback. He would have walked in his
bare feet, depending upon God and God's creatures to
nourish and protect him. During the second night of
Father Serra's walk to the city a venomous snake had bitten
him, and only a series of miracles had kept him alive until
he reached the convent at the outskirts of Mexico City. He
had accepted this disaster as a rebuke from God, and after
these many years he still suffered patiently from the injury
to his leg. It was a familiar misery to him now, but its
significance had remained clear to him.

When he reached the top of the hill he walked quietly
to his camp and prepared a meager breakfast—a dish of
corn-meal mush—over a small bed of charcoals, then made
plans for his day in the Indian village.

This would be a difficult day, for he had promised God
to bring at least one woman into the Church before sunset.

It would be a difficult day because women unnerved him
and he was never at his ease with them. They seemed—
even the Indian ones—less simple than the men, and although in the end they were hardier converts than the
men, he could not always understand how they arrived at
their belief. They did not climb a hill straight from its base
to its summit but arrived there along paths the priest did
not know at all. He could lead a man directly to the top,
but a woman he could only lead toward it and let her find
her own way. He was never certain she would find it. But
experience had taught him that once at the top she was unlikely to return to the valley and that she invariably had the
strength to bring her children out of the valley, too. How-

ever uncomfortable it made him, he must bring women into the Church this day.

Now he tried to think of the things that had interested the women of the Pamé Nation. One thing he knew. He could not approach women with an abstract conception of God. He had first to attract them with the concrete. From the concrete to the abstract the transition was not difficult. Frequently the women made it without this help.

Thinking in terms of the concrete, he decided first upon two large sacks of corn meal. Corn meal had become the most important food staple to the Pamé women after he had taught them how to make a dough and shape it into tortillas. Later he had planted seeds for them and they had watched the seeds become plants and ears of corn which they could grind into meal. That had been the first miracle to come from the white man's god. The planting of corn had changed their nomadic habits. It pleased them —both men and women—to watch the growth of their own corn, and they had learned man's eternal satisfaction in enjoying the fruits of their own labor. Yes, today, he would carry two sacks of corn meal and a few lumps of salt to flavor the dough.

A handful of bone needles and some coarse thread were next on his list. The needles had delighted the Pamé women, and the Indian boy had already requested one as a gift for his bride. Scissors. He owned two precious pairs of scissors; one of them he would take to the village.

Candles were important, for the soft light from the candles had seemed to be another miracle of the white man's god to the Pamés. He had only two—enough for a single chapel service—but he believed he should take one today.

He needed something else, however. He needed something that would give them a concept of the One True God. The cross was not enough, or rather it was too much. Like all men and women, they had far to go to learn the meaning of the cross. The priest pondered for a long time over this problem before he could reach a decision. He would show them the Child Jesus. The Child Jesus the Indian women would surely understand.

He removed from a heavy iron chest a fine porcelain figure clothed in exquisite silk garments. It was the sweet-faced Child Jesus that would occupy an important place near the altar in the chapel. It was a priceless piece of art but he was certain he would need it this day. He had so little time. After today—seven days at the most remained to him.

When he had assembled his offerings and had them packed into the saddlebags he realized he would have to lead them on his mule. He had not planned to ride the mule into the village. Indians who had not seen these strange animals were often frightened by them and he wanted no unnecessary trouble today. Nevertheless, the mule would have to go.

Before the sun had risen over the hill he was ready for his journey down the hill and through the forest to the river. He was troubled by the feeling that he had forgotten something and he delayed his departure while he reconsidered his load. Then he opened the iron chest again and removed a tiny leather bag. He would take this, too. Perhaps it was worldly and frivolous of him, but the golden earrings inside the bag seemed quite appropriate for the pretty girl—Francisco's girl. Yesterday she had worn a pair of crude earrings fashioned from what looked like a kind of soapstone. The golden ones would be more becoming to her. She would value them for their delicate beauty, he believed, for she would never understand their value in Spanish reales. He would ask Francisco to give them to her, however.

As he rode slowly down the hill through the short sea-pines and scrub oaks, the earth began to stir, to turn less silently upon its axis. From the stockade behind him circled wisps of smoke only a shade darker than the lifting fogs. Breakfast was being prepared in the camp for the men now shaking themselves into consciousness.

When the priest reached the forest the birds were ripping the silence with their early-morning calls and whistles, and across his path ran chipmunks and rabbits and squirrels. Of all the small animals of the forest Father Serra loved best the bright-eyed greedy little chipmunks who seemed to fear nothing so much as hunger. They amused him as the hummingbirds—bright and agile—amused him. They were greedy, too, as they flew from flower to flower, drinking only the best from each. As the brilliant-feathered birds flew past him, he wished that, like St. Francis, he could charm them closer to him. Nearsighted as he was, they were only red and green and purple and yellow arrows which, by their movement, he knew to be birds instead of flowers.

Once in the forest, he could no longer see the gold

verbena, the sea marigold, the thick chaparral, the silver sagebrush that covered the dry foothills. The sea was out of sight and the sun was visible only in patches as it shone through the long-coned sugar pine and the yellow pines, which were foreign to him, and the cottonwood trees—the álamos. In the occasional clearings that were small meadows he saw millions of golden poppies which the Spaniards called "cups of gold."

The mist was rising quickly now like a dozen or more thin curtains to reveal a gigantic stage. High and far away the priest saw the big and massive backdrop of the stage —another range of rounded yellow mountains. To reach San Diego he had crossed that range on this same weary mule and he knew what lay behind it: other magnificent ranges, other forests—all a part of the fresh, vigorous New World he would never be able to leave.

As the sun rose higher and the smell of the sunburned pines reached his nostrils and the sounds of the forest became louder and more distinguishable to his ears, Father Serra felt a familiar exaltation. He had felt it many times in his journey, but the frequency had not dulled its intensity. His heart beat furiously with his exaltation and he would have liked to praise the Creator of this sweet, wonderful world in song, and then he thought ruefully of his poor miserable voice. Such caterwauling would alarm even his lethargic mule.

A man might have only one moment like this in his life and still be grateful, he thought. Men lived through their lives to the end and did not experience one.

What kept them from such moments? Sometimes he

thought it was because they did not demand enough. They did not know they had a right to moments of complete ecstasy. Actually, man, greedy as he seemed to be, demanded little. He asked for a roof to keep away the rain—as well as the moon and the stars and the sun. He asked for little pieces of gold that had been dug out of the earth. He was satisfied with a piece of dead hog or cow when he might have asked for the finest fish and fowl. He was pleased to love one or two people and hate the rest, while the heart God gave him had room for the love of the whole world. Men did not want the Kingdom of Heaven on earth. Why they did not, Father Serra was never able to explain to himself. It was to remain a problem to him until the day he died.

And while he was thinking of these things he reached the river. The atmosphere had suddenly changed. It was not the intoxicating air of the hills and sea nor the cool sweet air of the forest, but the oppressive atmosphere of the lowlands. The sun was now beating directly upon him. . . . Then he saw a long row of giant bamboos. The Indian boy had told him that when he reached the bamboos he would be inside the village.

He guided his mule along the dry riverbank that was the village, past an assortment of huts similarly built, yet each with a distinguishing characteristic—a difference in the size of the door or the shape of the roof or the pattern of the woven tule that hung over the door opening.

When he reached the middle of the village he halted his

mule in front of a much larger building covered with earth and grass and brush so that, more than a house built by men, it resembled a low, rounded hill. This, the priest supposed, was the meetinghouse the Indian boy had described to him.

Such government as the village had was conducted from this place. The government was loosely organized under a single chieftain, the leader only because he was the ablest man of the community, and he was allowed to bequeath his job to his son only if the son was worthy of it. If the son did not prove himself to be the strongest and most fearless man of the village, he was "sung" out of his position and another was "sung" into his place. All problems of tribal importance were discussed in the meetinghouse by the village men and women, who had equal voices in their settlement.

Not far from the meetinghouse was a long, low building much larger than the other huts, but constructed in a similar fashion. This would be, Father Serra told himself, the sleeping place for the adult males. The boy had explained to him that after a secret initiation into manhood the males slept away from their homes in a communal dormitory. The girls, following their own painful and complex rites of puberty, remained in their homes.

Not worshiping a god, the Indians had no priest. Their shaman, who was doctor, prophet, and seer, conducted the burial services and other ceremonial rites and was the second man of importance in the village, but his house was no larger or finer than the others.

Riding his mule through the village Father Serra had passed a few Indian men who stared at him curiously. Those who had worked in the stockade greeted him, then continued to stare. Only from a distance, however, had he seen any women. Those who were scrubbing their leather garments on the rocks in the river had fled into their huts to watch him from the security of invisibility.

Again he noticed with pleasure that the women were modestly clothed, so modestly, he told himself again, that he could be happy if greater nudities were never seen among the Christian women in Mexico. Some of the women wore skirts and bodices of doeskin, while others wore doeskin skirts and bodices of rabbit fur. Most of them wore sandals, which were two pieces of deerskin bound around their feet with narrow thongs, and headbands adorned with glass stones and small brilliant feathers.

In front of the meetinghouse Father Serra climbed down from his mule and tied the beast to the low-hanging bough of a water maple. Already a crowd of Indian men and children had surrounded the priest and his mule, examining the load and asking questions he was not able to answer at all. When he had finally made one of the gentiles understand that he was seeking Boy-Whose-Feet-Are-Wings, the entire group walked along as his escort to the Indian boy's hut. In front of the house the group dispersed, most of them finding positions on the riverbank from which they might watch the mule and the white man who wore clothes like a woman.

Hearing activity uncommon so early in the morning, Francisco appeared from the rear of his house, his hands

filled with what Father Serra observed as a "great pan-
cake," and invited the priest to enter his house.

At the door, which was nothing but an opening protected by a tule screen, Father Serra stopped, made the
sign of the cross, and said solemnly, as if he were about to
enter his chapel, "Peace be to this house."

The house, constructed of boughs of trees haphazardly
selected and hewn, with a high, slanting roof of bulrushes,
was divided into two dark little rooms by a large tule screen
similar to the one hanging over the doorway.

The first room, the boy explained, was the sleeping place
of his mother. In one corner of the room on the dirt-cov-
ered floor was her bed—a pile of bulrushes with a thick
leather blanket thrown over them. Except for an intricately
woven basket in another corner and a kind of table holding
a few soapstone dishes and vessels, the room was quite
bare.

The second room was now the bedroom of the old chieftain, the Old Man of the Village, who since he had become
old and ill—hence, no longer a male—had been permitted
to sleep away from the sleeping-house. This room, too, was
bare of all furnishings except the floor bed and the bows
and arrows of varying sizes and colors and designs hanging
against the wall.

"You will speak a word of greeting to Man-of-the-
Strength-of-Many-Wildcats?" Francisco asked. "He is old.
He will see only a few more settings of the sun." The boy
spoke without grief.

An old man who looked to be too near death to watch
even the setting of this day's sun, lay on a pile of bulrushes

made softer by a thick layer of pine needles. His dark skin, the quality and color of leather worn paper thin, had taken the form of his fleshless bones.

Hastily Father Serra made the sign of the cross. It seemed to him there could be little life left in this old man. But when Francisco spoke to him his face folded into a smile, and in the smile the priest saw Francisco. He saw that such a lad as Francisco was this morning the old man had been many mornings ago.

With effort the old man then opened his eyes, and in his eyes the priest saw nothing of Francisco.

When men grow old, Father Serra reflected, their eyes hold nothing but history, for they lose the present and desire nothing of the future. What history lay in these lightless eyes? No stories of kings and wars and poets. No knowledge of inventions and contrivances of men and women. No recording of time by calendars and timepieces —only by the settings of the sun and the increase and decrease of the moon and the changes from the rainy season to what Francisco called the not-rainy season. A contracted world had been the world those eyes had seen: a world of life and death in an almost imperceptible corner of the world, a lifetime of mornings spent in fishing and hunting, a lifetime of evenings spent in fashioning bows and arrows and in carving utensils of delicate beauty and tools of fine edge. . . . And now the long shadow of death was falling across these eyes.

For a few minutes the old man and the young boy spoke in a language which to Father Serra was like the twittering of blue jays, and then the boy spoke to the priest.

"The old man welcomes you to his house and asks that you break your fast with the fish caught this morning and with the cake from the acorns my mother has just prepared."

Father Serra looked at the old man and his heart warmed toward him as it had warmed toward Francisco. He would like to save this soul before it left its temporal dwelling, he explained to the Indian boy. He would like to offer him the deathbed salvation provided for by the Church, if Francisco would interpret for him the meaning of salvation through the Lord Jesus Christ.

The boy spoke again to the old man, who listened to his words, then smiled at the priest, and shook his head. The words he spoke the boy translated for the priest.

"He is grateful to you, but he wishes to die as he was born, as his fathers and their fathers were born and died. Death that comes to us from the sea he hears willingly for the night is old and without comfort. He wishes to lie in the burial ground surrounded by gifts from his people. Since you are my friend, he will allow you to leave a gift to be buried with the others."

"I shall be honored to leave a gift," Father Serra said, and removing a small wooden cross that hung at his throat, he placed it in the old man's hands. This old man who once had the strength of many wildcats had never seen an object carved in this design, but it was a gift from a friend and his clawlike fingers closed tightly around it.

Again Father Serra made a sign of the cross and prayed that God would receive the old man's soul, which was lost only through ignorance and through the lack of diligence

on the part of Christians. Later he would bring the candle
and leave it to burn at the old man's side. The gentle light
might comfort a little this man who had lived his life comforted by the sun and the stars.

"A man of wisdom and honor, I know," Father Serra said
softly, following the boy through an opening which was
the back door of the hut. "He is not your father?"

"He is my father's father. My father, who would now be
chieftain, died many rainy seasons ago. For the past two
circles of the moon my father's father has lived here with
my mother, who takes care of him. My mother stands over
there where the women are grinding the acorns. I have
spoken to her of you and she will greet you, too. She has
no fear of you—only of your mule."

"What is her name?"

"Women-With-Laughing-Heart."

Except that the young slimness had gone from her figure,
the woman looked little older than the girls Father Serra
had seen under the cliff the day before. She was dressed
in the plain manner of Francisco's girl, but around her
neck she wore a necklace of tiny perfect shells set in an
enamellike substance, and her earrings were even smaller
shells set in the same black substance. Although she stared
solemnly at the priest, she did not have the tight look of
fear that showed itself in the faces of Indian women until
they had accustomed themselves to the sight of a white
man.

She left the women at the grinding stone and walked
over to the stone oven on which the acorn pancakes were
baking. She picked one up and offered it to Father Serra.

While he was eating it he asked Francisco to bring him the two sacks of corn meal from the saddlebags.

The woman did not take her eyes from him as he began to mix the corn meal with some water and a little salt. And when he had blended a fine dough and was slapping it into the shape of tortillas, the other women came to watch, standing as the girls had stood the day before—ready for flight should this strange man suddenly turn on them. Woman-With-Laughing-Heart was a daring one, for when the first tortilla was browned she accepted it from the priest and ate it—cautiously at first, then greedily. The flavor of corn and salt delighted her.

The women stepped nearer, still watching every movement the priest made. Another bold one accepted the second tortilla and when the third one was well toasted Father Serra was completely encircled by women who had lost their fear sufficiently to whisper to each other and giggle. These women looked curiously alike to him—as if they were all members of a single family, the only distinguishable ones being Woman-With-Laughing-Heart and the three sisters Francisco wished to marry.

For the next few minutes Father Serra was busy with his tortillas, and such was his earnestness and simplicity that he gave no thought to the strangeness of his conduct nor to the opinion the Bishop of Mexico might have of it. He was thinking only that he had been wise to bring the quantities of corn meal. When he had baked a tortilla for each of the women, there was enough meal left to give each of them a small amount. Francisco told them to go and fetch a vessel for the corn meal, which was a gift from the white man, and although they did not want to leave, they wanted the corn meal even more, and soon each had gone away and had hurried back with her boat-shaped vessel.

While they stood there, Father Serra told them where the corn came from and showed them a handful of seeds. One planted the seeds, he said, the corn grew tall and produced ears of corn. The corn, like the acorn, was ground into this fine meal.

The women stared. Was the white man a shaman? they asked Francisco, that he could plant the little seeds and grow the corn meal? Father Serra explained that it was indeed not the magic trickery of the shaman. Any of them could plant the seeds, which needed only air and water to nourish them—like the trees and the plants of the forest. If such a thing was a miracle, it was a miracle of the One True God.

"This god, then," they asked, "is he a shaman?"

The Indians never failed to ask this question: Is the white man's god a witch doctor? And now they waited, intent upon his reply, their soft, untroubled eyes fixed upon the mobile, deeply creased face of the white man's priest.

"God is not a shaman," he explained. "The shaman is no more than you or I or the baby in his mother's arms. God is the source of life and death. Nothing comes into the world or leaves it except through God. God is the thunderstorm that shakes the earth; He is the smallest leaf on the youngest álamo on the riverbank."

The women murmured softly among themselves and Francisco repeated their words to the Franciscan father.

"We understand the spirit that creates everything that

lives," he said. "But is not this spirit the enemy of death, who lives with the dead suns in the bottom of the sea and comes forth only to destroy?"

Father Serra shook his head. "God is life and death— one and the same—for without death there is no life. Everything begins to die as soon as it is born, yet death is the beginning of life for those who would live forever."

Again the women murmured and Father Serra knew they did not understand his words. Experience had taught him, too, that because they did not understand them they would stop listening to them, and that to hold their attention he must return quickly to the homely, partly familiar things.

He showed them his pair of scissors, the bone needles, and the coarse thread. With the scissors he cut into a length of soft doeskin Francisco had brought him and explained how easy it was to sew the pieces neatly together with a needle and thread.

Since he had only a handful of needles, he gave them to the older women and promised that when the great ship arrived there would be needles and thread for them all. They might even sew garments for their men, he said. This made the women laugh. Everybody knew that men did not wear garments—only the strange white men who came here from the sea.

While they laughed, one of the younger women pointed to Father Serra's spectacles and much against his judgment he removed them and gave them to her. She put them on and this time the women laughed without restraint. One after the other, they tried on the spectacles, giving the priest a difficult quarter of an hour. Even with them he was half blind; without them he was helpless. To his relief they came back to him unbroken.

Would these pieces of glass arrive on the big ship? the women asked. He explained that only very old men like himself wore them, but the women were less satisfied with his explanation even than Tomás had been. He laughed softly to himself. With a load of spectacles he could make easier conversions.

Like any good showman, when Father Serra felt the interest of his audience droop a little he moved on to a new diversion, and again like a good showman, he kept his important exhibition until the last.

The morning had spent itself and the sun stood almost directly above him when he opened a box and brought from it the beautiful figure of the Child Jesus.

He allowed them to look at it for many minutes before he spoke to them again. Their awe of the lovely figure wrapped in fine white silk was such that they did not try to touch it. They had never seen a figure made and clothed by man. One woman who held a nursing child in her arms drew close and spoke rapidly to Francisco.

"What does she want?" Father Serra asked.

"She believes it is a living child," Francisco replied, "she offers to suckle it."

With Francisco's help Father Serra explained the meaning of the figure. It was made in the image of the Son of God, who was born of a woman like all women's sons. The women listened, enchanted with his words. The white man's God was the father of the most beautiful baby in the world. Where was the baby of which this was the image? They would like to see the living child. The living child, Father Serra said, pointing to the cloudless sky, is now in the arms of the Great Father, the Father not only of the white men but of the brown and black and yellow men. Some day you may see Him face to face, he told them, for you do not have to die. Only those who choose death have to die.

He spoke earnestly and simply, and with like enthusiasm Francisco explained his words which had to do with baptism and conversion and the Church. Then when all the women were silent, standing worshipfully around the little figure, Father Serra left them and walked down to the spring to drink some water.

The oppressive midday heat had exhausted him. The sun, gimlet eyed, seemed to be directing its fiercest rays upon his back and shoulders. For the first time he could almost understand why the men who lived in the river valley refused to wear clothes. He washed his face with water from the spring, then sat down under a tree to rest for a moment.

The women still stood near the figure which Francisco's mother held tenderly in her arms. It was an impressive tableau, Father Serra thought. Now the women looked less alike to him, more like any group of women—women with love in their hearts. Gradually they separated into chattering groups, leaving only Francisco's mother and the three sisters with the figure of the Child Jesus. Again the priest bitterly regretted his inability to speak directly to them as well as his inability to see them clearly.

The face of the second sister was a sullen mask, and the priest wondered what—if anything—lay behind it. Her features were not unlike those of the youngest girl, yet she looked as Francisco's girl might look if she were ill—even as she might look when the life had gone out of her body. Her black clear eyes stared without seeming to see, and she listened as if she could not hear. Behind the smooth dark brow free from the narrow leather bands with which the other women held back their hair there was no apparent recognition of things nor understanding of people around her. The priest could not remember what the Indian boy had told him about the second sister except that she held a position of distinction in the village.

The lines of the priest's face deepened into a smile as he watched the oldest sister with the Child Jesus. She would be the Martha of the village, of course. Her face was a gentle caricature of her youngest sister's—the nose a little too long, the mouth much too wide for her thin face, the small black eyes too closely set together for beauty. Yet in her marriage arrangements she would be worth many seashells, for no other girl in the village was so skillful at making and repairing fishing nets nor so willing to give much time to the preparation of the daily fish stew.

Then suddenly the priest noticed a hurried movement among the women. He looked up and saw that they were crowding together to watch the approach of a group of men. They separated immediately, allowing the group headed by a short, heavy figure whose only apparel was a talo—a plumed headdress fastened to a leather band around his head—to pass through them on their way to the tree where the priest was resting.

Before the group of men had reached the tree, Francisco was standing beside the priest.

"The shaman comes to greet you," he explained. His voice, low and solemn, indicated the importance of this meeting.

Father Serra rose from his comfortable spot beneath the tree to receive the shaman's salutation.

"Man-Who-Dresses-Like-Woman is welcome to the village," the shaman said. Then he turned to Francisco and asked him to interpret his words for the white stranger.

"God's blessings upon you and the village, and greetings from his Majesty King Carlos of Spain," the priest replied. This meeting had a particular significance, he was certain, and he gave it his own kind of formality. The shaman had spoken words of welcome, yet his voice and manner were not friendly. Enmity from this source was not unexpected, however. The shamans everywhere had feared and hated the word of the True God. Father Serra looked carefully into the faces of the men who had accompanied the shaman. None of the converted gentiles were among them, although Tomás in his blue tunic and loincloth stood alone a short distance away.

"The white men have come to stay in the land of the Indians?" the shaman asked, and when Francisco had translated his words, the priest replied:

"The white men have traveled a great distance and at a great cost to find fertile soil and a place where they may spread the truth of God."

"Yet," the shaman insisted, "for as many suns as there have been, it has been the home of the dark men."

"Tell him," the priest said to the Indian boy at his side, "that in this wonderful land there is room for many men. The soil is rich and the forests and waters are abundant. They should be at the disposal of all men. It is, moreover, the will of God that His truth be known to all people. That is the important thing."

Again the shaman spoke to Francisco:

"Explain to me what Man-Who-Dresses-Like-Woman means by the truth."

"His truth," the Indian boy said glibly," is belief in the white man's god. There is only one god. He lives in the sky. He watches over all of us—even the birds in the forests and the fish in the sea."

"And how does he speak to men?" the shaman asked.

The boy pondered for a moment and then replied:

"He speaks through the great bell which is to hang on top of the white man's church. When he speaks, he can be heard all over the earth."

Then the shaman had his question directed to the priest.

"The truth," he asked, "you know it and you speak it?"

The priest's voice—astonishingly loud and resounding from so small a man—was challenging.

"Yes," he said. "It has been given to me to know the truth and I would speak it to God's creatures everywhere."

When Francisco had interpreted the reply—in his own fashion—the shaman, his eyes fixed upon the priest's, made a circling gesture with his arm to the man who stood directly behind him. The man stepped forward with a large pottery cup which he put into the shaman's hands. Then he returned to his position behind the witch doctor.

The shaman held the cup out to the priest, and again Francisco listened to the witch doctor. This time he hesitated for a moment before he repeated the Indian's words in Spanish.

"We offer a drink of the dark men to Man-Who-Dresses-Like-Woman. May it refresh him," the shaman had said.

Father Serra's long, almost fleshless fingers closed around the cup. He looked at its black tealike contents, thinking he had never seen a less appetizing liquid. He was so tired from the long morning of standing that his legs and hands trembled a little. With a tremendous effort he steadied his hands while he looked into the cup. The sun was throwing its heat across his back and shoulders, and little streams of sweat trickled down his back.

The crowds—the men and the women, too—were strangely silent, and without looking away from the drink in his hands the priest felt every eye of the village directed toward him. For a moment it seemed to him that the village had stopped breathing while it waited for him to drink from the shaman's cup.

Still uncertain, he glanced at Francisco, whose face until that moment had been without expression. In reply to the priest's unvoiced question, the Indian boy smiled and said, "Drink it, padre."

In one swallow Father Serra drank the bitter oily liquid and tried to keep a grimace from his face as he returned the empty cup to the shaman.

Still the men and women stood silent and motionless—

as if they would never move or speak again. Still they kept their eyes fixed upon the white man.

The priest wiped the sweat from his forehead and half turned to sit down again in the shade of the willow tree, but the unwavering silence of the villagers kept him standing there—waiting—although he did not know what he waited for. Sickened now by the drink, he could not think. He wanted only to lie down under the tree. But he was unable to take the steps that would make it possible. He was imprisoned in the web of silence these people wove tighter and tighter around him.

It was the shaman himself who finally broke through the web. A few minutes later—minutes that had the quality of hours—the shaman muttered a few words to his companions and handed the pottery cup to the man who had carried it. Then with no further word to the priest nor to the other Indians he turned and walked away, followed by the men who had accompanied him. Father Serra was not certain, but it seemed to him that if there was any expression on the shaman's face it was one of disappointment.

As soon as the shaman had left the enclosure that encircled Francisco's house, the women began to whisper and then to talk and giggle hysterically. The web of silence had completely vanished.

The priest spoke to Francisco. "If you will guide me to my mule," he said, "I will return to the camp. There is surely no more for me to do here today."

"You are well, padre?" Francisco asked.

"Of course, quite well," the priest answered sharply.

Except, he added to himself, for this nausea in my stomach.

"The women," Francisco said, as if he had forgotten the visit of the shaman, "it was very strange listening to them. They believe you are perhaps more than a shaman, and they loved the Child Jesus."

"What do they say, boy?" Father Serra asked. "You think they wish to be baptized?"

The boy did not reply.

The priest limped across the road and with Francisco's help he was able to climb on the back of his mule.

"If that is their desire," he continued, "let them come to the chapel tomorrow morning, Francisco. First I shall give them instruction, then they may be baptized."

"You will give them Spanish names?"

"Yes."

"There may be many."

"There is an abundance of names for them, boy," the priest said impatiently.

"The best names must be kept for the sisters and my mother," Francisco insisted. "Should they wish to be baptized," he added.

"Very well, Francisco. They shall have the best names of the Christian world. And what of you, boy? You wish to be baptized so that you may truly bear the name of St. Francis?"

The boy shook his head and the priest said no more. The image of the Child Jesus had not been enough for this boy, nor had anything the priest said been enough. Only a deep conviction would move him to the Church, and Father

Serra did not know at all how he could bring this conviction to him.

Right now he could not think about it. He was desperately ill. The important thing was to get out of the village.

He rode slowly through the quiet empty village, the nausea in his stomach rising in waves to his throat, then receding only to rise again, but he forced the sickness back until he reached the row of giant bamboos. Once in the forest he gave way to the weakness and, half falling from his mule, he collapsed on the soft grayish moss beneath the trees. . . .

When his consciousness returned he was lying on the riverbank and a dark-skinned hand was washing his face with a piece of blue cotton cloth. He looked down with disgust at the front of his robe. During his unconsciousness he had vomited the contents of the shaman's cup. Almost too weak to care what was happening to him he raised his eyes to the face close to his. It was the stolid countenance of the third sister, the Indian girl with the strange, blank eyes.

She laid the wet cloth on his forehead and held a cup to his lips, urging him to drink from it. Although this liquid was more bitter than the shaman's he was unable to protest. Then with quick, realistic gestures she showed him that he must vomit again. Three times and with great haste she repeated the treatment. Finally she poured a gaseous liquid down his throat that cooled and soothed his stomach. As soon as he had swallowed it, she vanished.

Painfully the priest turned his eyes to see what had happened to the girl, but she had apparently gone back to the village. For two hours he lay exhausted and half asleep upon the cool rushes of the riverbank, and then as if by a miracle he suddenly felt rested and restored. He stood up and walked toward his patient mule, which was waiting for him. He rubbed his aching eyes, then gasped for breath, and ran in a panic back to the riverbank. Then he drew in a deep breath of relief. His spectacles were lying on the piece of blue cloth stretched over a rock.

When he reached the wide clearing halfway between the village and the camp, he saw two men coming toward him on horseback, obviously on their way to the village. Not until they had almost passed him did Father Serra recognize them. One was the fair-haired Viamonte and the other was the corporal, Figueroa.

"Where would you go?" he asked Viamonte.

"To the village," Viamonte replied gaily. "The comandante tells us you wish to establish friendly relations with the heathen natives. We are on our way . . . to establish friendly relations." The corporal laughed.

"You do not speak their language," the priest said.

"It does not matter. One does not need to speak a language to establish friendly relations, does one, corporal?" Again the corporal laughed.

"There must be no trouble," Father Serra insisted.

"You lack faith in us, padre. You astonish me. We wish only to be friends with the people."

"Go, then, with God," Father Serra replied, urging his mule forward.

He did not like it. Viamonte was a man without a single intention of friendliness, and the corporal was without in-

tentions of any kind. He was no more than a follower and
a rather bad liar. For a moment the priest thought of returning to the village, and then decided against it. This
relationship between the white man and the brown man
must be settled sooner or later. Besides, he had complete
confidence in Francisco's ability and determination to protect his people.

His early-morning exaltation had left him. Now as he
rode through the forest he was just an old and weary man,
his thoughts far from the beauty of his surroundings.

He reflected upon his morning's work. He had interested
the women, he was certain, but he did not have the conviction that he had persuaded them away from their belief
in a few superstitions taught them by their shaman to a
belief in the True God. It was possible that he had persuaded the one sister. She had apparently followed him
from the village, prepared to help him. How had she
known he was ill?

For the first time the thought came into his mind that
the shaman might have tried deliberately to poison him.
He had long been accustomed to strange, vile-tasting
drinks prepared and enjoyed by the Indians, and it had not
occurred to him that the shaman would be pleased to see
him dead. Perhaps without the help of the girl he would
have died in the forest. The thought terrified him—not the
thought of violent death, for he had always expected to die
of some form of violence, but he was not ready to die. Too
much work still lay before him.

Then—as he was always able to do—he dismissed the

shaman from his mind and directed it to what was yet to be accomplished.

The rest of the day, he told himself, he must devote to the Spaniards and their personal problems. In his preoccupation with the Indians he too often forgot the character of Spanish adventurers. They were always eager to do battle where they were or to move elsewhere or to return to their homes, but they were never content with an unchanging situation.

He hoped, too, that he might persuade a few of them to join him in his prayers for the return of the *San Antonio*. He wanted no fainthearted, disbelieving men to pray with him but some, or even one, who believed as he did. He knew that on this, the second day, no one believed. He also knew that such a faith could come to any of them.

At midnight he was again alone on his knees beneath the cliff. Peace had come once more to his little place on earth. The dark quiet hours of the night satisfied the Franciscan father. Although he realized that men used the darkness of these hours to conceal the evil things they did, he preferred not to think of those things. He liked to believe that men were sleeping in peace wherever darkness covered the earth, and that God was content with them.

The Third Day

The Third Day

PIERCED HERE and there by swiftly vanishing stars, the western sky was still black and the white foam of the waves that rolled over the beach was only faintly touched with a translucent pink from the rising sun when Father Serra closed his morning prayers and returned to the chapel on the hill.

He walked softly, for the camp still slept, and the only sounds were the customary sea sounds these men slept by. Before long the men who, tired and sober, had gone to their beds shortly after sunset would be moving about in their camps, their naked bodies sweating even before the sun touched the company area, while those who had spent the hours until well after midnight gambling and drinking brandy in the officers' camp would sleep until heat and thirst forced them out of their beds. But now even the cooks who would soon be stirring corn meal in the great iron pots of boiling salt water for the breakfast atole were still comfortably unaware of the rising sun.

When the priest reached the chapel, the young Indian boy was already waiting for him, eager for the beginning of this important day. His usually tranquil voice was impatient with the restraint of foreign words.

"The women of the village have risen early," he said, "to

prepare themselves for their visit to the stockade. Now
they wait for me to return and accompany them here.
What I wish to ask you is this: shall their men come too,
armed with their bows and arrows?"

"Why should their men come armed to the stockade?"
the priest asked.

"I feared the white men might make trouble for the
women."

"I trust there was no trouble in the village yesterday,"
Father Serra said, inviting the boy with a wave of his hand
to sit down beside him on Manuel's bench.

"No, there was no trouble. Why?"

"As I left, I met Viamonte riding into the village. It was
in my mind that he might attempt to molest the women."

Francisco laughed. "The man with the yellow hair and
his friend came to the village to speak with the girls, but
there were no girls."

"What do you mean?"

"I caused them to vanish. When the white men reached
the village they found only men resting on the riverbank,
their bows and arrows within reach of their hands, and
many old women sleeping in the sun. The children were
playing in the river, but the girls had vanished. The white
men were not diverted by these old women and men and
children, and they soon rode out of the village."

"Where do your people go when they vanish?" the priest
asked curiously.

"An Indian can disappear so that not even another
Indian can find him," the boy said. "He becomes a part of
the forest. But I must tell you the girls did not vanish

willingly. They looked upon the man with hair like the sun and wondered if he was not the god you spoke of yesterday. They feared him, yet they did not wish to go away."

"Why would they believe that Viamonte is God?"

"It lies in the memory of every Indian that one day godlike men shall appear out of the sea. Their skin will be white and their hair will be like the rays of the sun."

The priest looked up at the changing sky. Even yet the sun behind the hill was not visible. He thought of Viamonte, whose voice was the most profane of them all during these nights of gambling and drinking. Viamonte, whose heart was dark and confused with many hatreds, would, to be sure, appear like a god to these small dark people. The golden-haired Viamonte with his beardless, angelic face, his extraordinary blue eyes, his sharp arrogance, had doubtless charmed many a savage into such a belief. A pity, Father Serra thought, that he was not a more godlike man. He might have served the Church well. As it was, he served only himself—and without grace.

These mysterious race memories of the Indians only abetted such arrogance as Viamonte's, and such arrogance was the sin of the world, Father Serra told himself. Without arrogance, what evil could there be? What was the origin of the arrogance of the white-skinned man and why was it so shamelessly unquestioning and unquestioned? How had it come about that a man could describe the color of his skin and say "this makes me the master of other men"? How had he succeeded in making other men believe this?

This white-skinned arrogance was not the only arrogance. There was the arrogance of the possessor of things, and at the other end the arrogance of the possessor of nothing, for St. Francis had often to admonish his disciples: "Take no pride in your poverty. Accept no praise for your humility" . . . The arrogance toward the aged of the young who never believe they will grow old . . . the arrogance of the living toward the dead, for what miserable living sinner does not feel superior, in living, to the great, dead saints, and what living coward does not feel bolder than the dead heroes? . . . Arrogance in religion and in physical strength and in knowledge . . . These were the arrogances of the Spaniards, and the victim was simple goodness. Simple goodness could not hold itself against the arrogance the Spaniards brought with them to the New World. Its only protection was the Indians' animallike fear of the unknown. Such a fear, along with Francisco's instinctive awareness of Viamonte's nature, had guarded his people the day before.

The Indian boy had climbed to the top of the wall and was looking down to the sea. The pink of the foam had reddened, and the waves approaching the shore in straight lines collapsed like the shuffling of a gigantic deck of cards. The boy jumped from the wall and then lay flat on the ground to watch the change of the western sky from gray to blue. Only one star was now visible and in a few minutes it would vanish, too. The priest marveled how the boy had achieved his position almost in a single movement. Civilized man had come far from the animal's economy of activity.

"Explain to me," the boy said, "what you will tell the

women. I know what you have said to the men you have baptized, but they are words without meaning."

"I shall tell them that they must be born again—as you say the sun is born again each day."

"They must return to the creator in the hills and then to the bellies of their mothers?"

"Not their bodies. It is their souls that must be born again."

"What is this soul?"

"It is a spirit within you. It is the spirit that makes man different from the fish in the sea and the animals of the forest."

"How is it born again?" the boy asked.

"It must go before God and become as a small child free from sin. It must confess its sins before it is born again."

"What are these sins?"

Father Serra thought for a moment before he answered. "The sins of greed, of having other gods than the One True God, of false witnessing," he said.

"I do not understand these sins."

"Well," the priest explained, "marriage with more than one woman is a sin. Killing a man or woman is a sin. But above all it is necessary to believe in the One God and to abandon all others."

"The Indians have no gods."

"Then they must learn that there is One God and they must believe in His power and goodness."

"These things you will explain to the women before you baptize them?"

The priest sighed. "I shall try to do this, yes, boy."

"And their names!" The boy sat up and clasped his knees with his arms. "I wish to listen when you give them their names. Which is the best of all the names?"

The priest answered this time without hesitation.

"María," he said.

"Why is this the best?"

"María was the name of the mother of the Son of God, the mother of the Child Jesus. María was also the name of a girl who loved Jesus very much and spent her time with him wisely. Then, too, it was the name of a woman who sinned and loved and repented."

"María," the boy said softly, "that must be kept for the one I shall marry. María."

"The pretty little one."

"Yes, she must be María. You must not give this name to the women you baptize today, padre, but keep it for my wife—should she make up her mind to be baptized."

"And her sisters who would be baptized today?"

"What are other good names?"

Again the priest was thoughtful. "There was Marta," he said. "She was not so pretty as María nor so wise. Yet she cooked well for the Master and saw that He was well taken care of."

"Let that be the name of the oldest sister, whose face is not beautiful but who is more skillful than any with the fish and the pancakes."

"Very well. She shall be Marta. And what about the third one? What name shall we save for her?"

"She is the foolish one. The words that come from her

mouth often do not make sense. That is because she is occupied by the spirit of another. This one is sacred to my people. No one dares touch her until she is married, and she will cost her husband many more clam shells than her two sisters—even though she is not beautiful and the young men of the village have fear of her. She was not even compelled to suffer the rites of puberty because my people feared that the hot stones used to soften the girls' thighs might drive away the spirit."

"What is she like—the foolish one?"

"She is the singer of the village. There has never been one like her. She sings of everything. She sings of the sea where death is and of the mountains where life begins. She sings of the sun and the stars and the moon. And she sings of little things like the fishing nets and the river rafts, of the bear cubs and the smallest flowers on the river bank. All my people sing, but when the foolish one sings everybody stops to listen, for she sings with the voice of the other spirit that lives in her. What she sings is true."

"Santa Cecilia," the priest murmured. "Let her be Cecilia. Making music from the spirit within her was Santa Cecilia's second love. I cannot be certain this girl is really foolish. It was her common sense that saved my life . . ." The priest paused and looked sharply at the boy. "Did you know your shaman was trying to poison me?"

"That was not his intention, padre," the boy said. "He wished to prove that you were telling the truth or that you were not telling the truth."

"And if I had fallen dead?"

"That was not possible. You see, I knew that. I knew you spoke your truth."

* * *

It was a difficult morning. In terms of homely things, Father Serra tried to explain to the women the significance of the Church, of conversion and baptism, but the women failed to understand him and, although they smiled and agreed with what he said, their attention quickly turned to the figure of the Child Jesus, the candles, the altarcloth, and the silk garments that clothed the lovely figure of the Virgin Mary.

Father Serra had faced this difficulty before and, as he had done in the past, he forced himself to be content with a meager accomplishment. He would win the people by the visible, the tangible, and the decorative, praying at the same time that someday the symbols would take on a deeper significance for them. He wondered, too, if his task would not have been easier if these people had worshiped false gods—gods that could be destroyed to give way to belief in the One True God. Or if they had followed barbarous customs that he could attack as contrary to the rights of men, substituting for them the praiseworthy customs of the Church.

Actually, the Indians of San Diego followed few tribal customs which had no place in the Church. They condemned, as a tribe, murder, robbery, falsification, and fornication, and only in the disgusting puberty rites and the customs of purchasing wives and taking more than one woman in marriage could Father Serra find these people in opposition to his own standards of behavior. Looking upon their serene, joyous faces this morning, he was conscious of only a feeble conviction of sin for them. The feebleness of this conviction troubled him, and while he instructed the women he searched his own soul for a lessening of faith not in God but in the interpretations of God that he had never questioned.

At midday he led his happy, chattering flock to the camp area, where bowls of atole and pieces of jerked beef were prepared for them. After their baptism in the afternoon they would take communion, but he had determined not to ask them to fast. Later he would explain the significance of abstinence to them, but abstinence in itself was no novelty to these women whose skin lay as close to their bones as his own. The good atole, he assured himself, would teach them a more practical and durable lesson.

After he had eaten his own meal he retired to his camp, tired and not completely satisfied with his morning's work. He was always painfully conscious at these times of the superficial quality of his instruction, and before he lay down on his bed for a brief rest he prayed that God would forgive his shortcomings. He missed his usual midday visit to the sea, which never failed to comfort him.

An hour later he rose and, in spite of the heat that soaked his clothing with sweat, felt invigorated by his short sleep. Now he must baptize the women and give them their Spanish names, remembering to keep for Francisco's bride the beloved name of María.

When he stepped out of his camp he pushed his spectacles back into place, and looked over the camping area.

The soldiers and colonists, curious about the Indian women, stood in groups around them, trying with no success to make them understand what they said.

Not far from Father Serra's camp a rabbitskin blanket had been spread flat on the ground and on it were kneeling two Indian women and five of Portolá's Leather Jackets. The women were laughing, and as he approached the group he recognized Francisco's mother, Woman-With-Laughing-Heart. Not until he was close enough to be a part of the group did he see that the five men and two women were playing a game.

He stood watching the game for a few minutes before he realized they were playing the ancient game of dice. However, these were not the Spanish dice of the soldiers, but a set of six two-sided dice, shaped like coins, which the Indian women must have brought from the village. When the dice fell upon the blanket, he saw crude pictures of heavenly bodies and fish and animals sketched on the sides. Heaped in front of the soldiers as well as the women were small piles of clam shells. One of the kneeling soldiers glanced up at the priest and laughed. "The stakes are clam shells," he explained. "The women have no interest in our silver reales."

After a few minutes the priest moved away, shrugging his shoulders. The game of chance was a universal language, indeed, for it was spoken in every corner of the world. Clam shells, silver coins, beads, gold coins—the game varied only in the medium of exchange. And those who played it had no trouble in understanding each other.

Then his eyes were attracted by a glittering object that seemed to draw the hot sun's rays directly upon it. As he approached this object, he saw that it was the bright yellow hair of Miguel Viamonte who with Comandante Portolá and some other officers had surrounded a group of young girls.

Among them the three sisters stood staring almost like a single unit: the little one, the foolish one, and the homely oldest one. It was as if the Spaniard's yellow hair had bewitched them all. Then suddenly and as swiftly as a bird the foolish one moved toward Viamonte, and stretching out her hand she touched his soft, shining hair.

Surprised by the intimate gesture, Viamonte seized her hand and tried to bring her closer to him, but the girl, full of fear then, pulled her hand away and hurried back to her sisters. The little one spoke sharply to her, then led her two sisters across the clearing to Woman-With-Laughing-Heart, who was still busy with her dice and a growing pile of clam shells.

Viamonte watched them in silence for a long time, his eyes finally fixing themselves upon the small one whose words the others obviously listened to. She could scarcely be fifteen years old, yet like all young girls of hot climates, she was indeed already a woman. Her soft doeskin bodice and skirt did not conceal her slim, rounded hips and well-filled breasts.

"Her Creator has formed her breasts and thighs like an artist," Viamonte said in a loud voice. "They give me the desire to amuse myself with her."

"With whom?" Portolá asked.

"With the little one, of course. The others are too scrawny for the taste of a Viamonte."

"Father Serra tells me she is the promised bride of the Indian boy you encountered yesterday."

Viamonte was still watching the girl who now sat by Woman-With-Laughing-Heart. Then his eyes turned speculatively toward the girls who stood near him. He shook his head as if they had been offered to him and he was refusing them.

"The little one," he said to Portolá, "could make a man forget his wife."

"You will have to take care," the comandante said. "The Indian boy is Father Serra's favorite, and the girl certainly belongs to the boy."

"A priest and a couple of savages have never alarmed me," Viamonte replied.

*　　*　　*

The baptism of the Indian women was less solemn than the Bishop of Mexico would have liked, Father Serra told himself, yet he was not displeased with it himself. One woman giggled when the baptismal water touched her forehead, and the somewhat hysterical sound set off a tittering which did not stop until Francisco spoke sharply to them. Their new names amused them, too, and Father Serra thought he had never heard such a babbling—certainly not since he had baptized a large number of women in the Pamé Nation. And they were curious about the chapel. Although they touched nothing, they examined every strange object with care, and they looked so long at the handsome altarcloth that the priest would not have been astonished if they had tried to make off with it.

He had instructed Francisco that with the final benediction the women should quietly leave the chapel, after genuflecting in the direction of the altar. But such an orderly departure did not satisfy the women, for they were not yet ready to leave.

"The women are like mosquitoes," Father Serra said to Francisco when one group of women left the chapel only to return to see why the others were still lingering. "One frees oneself from one only to be pestered by another."

Francisco laughed. He knew that the padre was pleased by the women's insistent interest, and he made no effort to persuade the women to go home until they had completely exhausted themselves.

*   *   *

At sunset Father Serra walked down to the sea and spread his cloak on the sandy shore. In a few minutes, the Indians would say, the sun would die. It would sink into the ocean and become just one more dead sun on the floor of the ocean. It was such a simple way to explain the disappearance of the most important heavenly body. Father Serra wondered for a moment why he endeavored to make it more difficult for them. Then he chided himself. He was giving way too often to the softening influence of this gentle land.

He needed a friend he could discuss these things with, in that manner strengthening himself in his faith. God alone was not enough for a mortal man. At the end of a long, difficult day a man, even a priest, needed a human friend to talk with, for this was the lonely time of the day—the time after achievement or lack of achievement. Then he reminded himself that this was the small price the missionary fathers often paid for the privilege of working in foreign lands—the small price of loneliness.

His thoughts turned to his beloved friend Palou and he realized how comforting it would be to have Palou with him in New California. Palou had accompanied him from the island of Mallorca to the New World and now he recalled their many long conversations together—their serious talk as well as their spirited, lighthearted gossip about the worldly affairs of the Church.

Father Palou was the second most important priest of the Church in Mexico, for in the event of Father Serra's death he would be appointed president-father of the missions of New California. Father Serra was sorry the Church had not been able to spare him for this expedition, and yet it was comforting to know that Father Palou was in Mexico, waiting to hear from him and certain to send him whatever he needed for his Indians. Only a man like Palou would understand the desperate need for such apparently trivial things as candles and incense and bone needles.

It had been Father Serra's good fortune that when he was a young priest in Mallorca, with no other desire in his heart than to travel to the West Indies, he had made a novena to the Virgin and to St. Francis, asking for the privilege of converting pagan souls and for a companion whose heart was filled with the same passionate desire.

The fortunate answer to this novena had been a call to the West Indies in the company of a young and equally eager priest, Father Palou. They were to take the place of two friars who had been enlisted in a company of priests to travel to the West Indies but who had withdrawn their enlistments because of fear of the sea.

From the day of their departure they had occupied themselves with the task to which they were dedicated. They had labored to save the souls of the heretic captain and his crew. At Puerto Rico, where they had stopped to take on water and had been delayed by a storm for two weeks, they had set up a mission and the twenty friars had scattered themselves all over the city to take it by storm with homilies and pious ejaculations. Puerto Rico had been one of their greatest triumphs, for they had not left one soul there unconfessed.

Since those first days Father Palou had been his closest companion and, although they were not always together, they had the assurance that within a few days they might see each other again and share their experiences, making them a part of their rich and varied past, which was certainly a past they held in common, the one never quite knowing where his own ended and the other's began.

Now Father Serra did not know when he would see his friend again, and he was lonely for him. Tomorrow, he promised himself, he would write Father Palou a long letter. After tomorrow only six days would be left for him here.

❊ ❊ ❊

The early evening stars came out sparingly, then profligately, crowding the skies with their pointed brilliance. Except for the waves that curled against the shore the Pacific was unmitigated darkness, but the rolling of the far-out sea swell made antiphonal music with the breaking of the waves, and although Father Serra could not see far beyond the shore, he felt the endlessness of the black waters.

Then suddenly out of the hills that had been silent he heard unfamiliar sounds, and he wondered if he had gone to sleep on his knees and had dreamed the sounds. At first he heard the shrill screams of women, alternating with dissonant notes from what might have been a flute. After a few minutes he recognized a pattern to the sounds—the women were singing in the high key of the flutes to the tempo of the rattles and drums.

As hastily as he could he made his way up the hill to the stockade and found that the comandante had already alerted the Leather Jackets, who moved like giant shadows through the dark clearing.

From the top of the wall near the cannons that faced the forest, a guard was shouting down his observations to Gaspar de Portolá.

"The fire in the center grows no higher," he said, "nor is the row of firebrands longer. At this moment it seems to be a ceremonial rite, for I can see small figures moving in and out of the light from the fire in rhythm with the singing. I can distinguish no drums, yet I hear distinctly drumlike sounds."

"Do the lights of the firebrands move in this direction?" Portolá asked.

"They do not seem to move except in a circle which breaks, then moves in a straight line only to form a circle again," the guard replied.

While he spoke the voice of one woman rose above the confusion of sounds and for a few minutes all the noise subsided and the guard stationed on the wall reported that the activity in the village had ceased, too. The woman's words were indistinguishable and her song was monotonously limited to four or five musical notes, but it was obviously a song of lamentation, sung with a poignancy of tone that Father Serra had never heard in a human voice. The soldiers of the camp listened in silence. For minutes nothing could be heard but the woman's sorrowful voice against the persistent roar of the sea.

"The Old Man of the Village," Father Serra whispered to the comandante when the song ended and the drumming and rattling were heard again. "The old chieftain must have died." He made the sign of the cross and murmured "Requiescat in pace."

"What meaning can his death have for us?" Portolá asked.

"I cannot be sure. According to the tribal custom, Boy-Whose-Feet-Are-Wings will be named chieftain."

"That is well for us, is it not?" the comandante asked impatiently. "The Indian boy is our friend."

"Yes, he is our friend."

When Father Serra had retired to his camp, the comandante ordered four Leather Jackets to ride to the edge of the village and to remain there until dawn unseen by the Indians.

*   *   *

All night Father Serra sat at his table lighted by a small oil lamp, and in his fine, careful script wrote letters to his friends and made notes of the day's events in his diary. The longest letter was addressed to Francisco Palou. Parts of this letter were concerned with his personal needs and those of his Indians, other parts with his own affection for the Indians of San Diego.

"We still never have enough candles and incense, I am afraid," he wrote. . . . "When we have established missions all the way from San Diego we shall need perhaps a dozen church bells. I cannot tell you how I miss the sweet tolling of the bells. . . . Although I still have one habit in fair condition, the old one is ruined by wear and weather, and I have quite finished with the many handkerchiefs I brought with me. When the next ship sails to our port here, I have confidence you will remember the candles and the handkerchiefs. . . . I cannot praise too highly the conduct of the gentiles. Their beautiful figure, deportment, affability, and joyousness have enamored all of us who have hearts, though you can be sure—a group of Spaniards of this proportion—there are some without God's love in their hearts. . . ."

*   *   *

All night the men in the camping area moved about restlessly, for the singing and the wailing from the village continued even after the sun had come up over the hill.

All night Gaspar de Portolá walked in circles inside the stockade, never leaving for long the guard who reported to him constantly from the wall. He had lost many men from the sea plague; he did not propose to lose any through carelessness. But he did not share Father Serra's confidence in the pacific intentions of these or any Indians.

The Fourth Day

The Fourth Day

"*Per omnia saecula saeculorum . . . Dominus vobiscum . . . Benedicamus Domino . . .*"

Father Serra spoke the concluding words of the Mass with reverent conviction. Even after all the years of countless repetition, the holy words of prayer and blessing held deep significance for him. He had struggled long for that eloquence and here again a human weakness had in part motivated the struggle. As a novice in the convent of San Bernardino he was so slight of body he could not reach the choir rack nor could he help his companions in the everyday labors of the Mass. Determined to be of meaningful service to God in spite of his physical weakness, he dedicated himself to the spoken word and as a young man was distinguished for his eloquence even among eloquent people. After making his vows he began to grow in strength but he was never to reach more than a medium stature. His power with words, however, intensified itself with his age. With it he could charm a French or Spanish bishop as easily as he could charm an Indian with his genuine devotion to him and his people.

Now as he spoke the words he looked down at the soldiers and colonists who in greater numbers than on any previous day were kneeling on the chapel floor. He could distinguish them easily enough, for the early-morning sun glittered on their bearded faces. But he saw with some anxiety that among them were none of the converted gentiles who, since their baptism, had not failed to attend the morning and evening services. He wondered if in their deep concern with the traditional rites of the tribe they had already forgotten their new God.

Thoughtfully he walked into the sacristy and was removing his vestments when he heard the shrill voice of an Indian call to him:

"Padre, padre, speak with Tomás!"

He put on his best robe, which was frayed at the hem from constant contact with the sandy soil, and hurried to open the door that led into the still-unpaved courtyard.

The gentile Tomás, his dark face sweating from the long run to the hilltop, spoke urgently in his awkward Spanish. Boy-Whose-Feet-Are-Wings had sent him with a message to the priest. The padre should accompany Tomás to the village.

"The Old Man is dead?" Father Serra asked. Without waiting for an answer he closed his eyes and whispered, "May he rest in peace."

"Dead, yes, dead." The Indian's voice was thin with the excitement of the preceding night and the importance to him of this moment. "The people ask for Man-Who-Wears-Dress-of-Woman and Man-Whose-Hair-Is-the-Sun."

The priest looked at Tomás with astonishment. "They ask for Viamonte?"

"Man-Whose-Hair-Is-the-Sun," Tomás repeated slowly, pointing toward the big Spaniard who was sitting inside a circle of sunlight in front of the chapel. "Maybe he is the new god, the god of the white man. Some of my people ask if this is true." Still looking at Viamonte, he added, "Tomás will return now to the edge of the village and wait for the white men." It did not occur to him that the priest might refuse to come. The old chieftain was dead; the command of Boy-Whose-Feet-Are-Wings would not be disobeyed.

Father Serra pushed his spectacles hard against the bridge of his nose, for only in that manner could he see an object from a distance of a yard, and watched Tomás vanish over the brow of the hill. He stared for a long time after the dark figure had disappeared. The Indian's words disturbed him. He did not want to add to his already difficult work the complication of a rival god in the form of the ungodlike colonist. Nor did he wish to deny his young friend's request.

*   *   *

Father Serra could not keep from admiring the powerful, well-built figure of Miguel Viamonte, who rode ahead of him through the forest with the sureness of a man conscious that he is a master of all things, but at the same time the priest wondered at the lavishness of God's gifts upon this man in whose face past sins and present weaknesses in no way revealed themselves. The man was a sinner, unrepentant except in formal, occasional confession, yet his blue eyes reflected good will. Though arrogant in his way of walking and riding, the arrogance did not show in his smile nor in his voice, and only by knowing the man had Father Serra discovered that greed and lust were his motivating forces. Greed, the ancient sin of the Spaniards, and lust, which was always second to greed.

The Indians, with all their sensitiveness to danger, perceived in the golden-haired Spaniard not the enemy but the image of a supreme being latent in their race memory. That had happened in Mexico, too, Father Serra reminded himself, two centuries before. The tradition of a fair-skinned race of gods, stirring deep through layers of memory, had betrayed the Aztecs and had made it possible for a handful of Spaniards to conquer a rich and well-defended nation. Across tropical swamps and barren mountains and fertile plains the Spaniards had marched, leaving no spot free from the marks of their heavy boots, and the Aztec princes, wearing fragile robes and golden sandals, had accepted these men as gods. Through the years the Spaniards had continued to march and the Indians, knowing that they were not gods but men with strange ambitions, had continued to retreat. The Spaniards still marched, Father Serra knew, and now as he thought of Miguel Viamonte, he remembered that this Spaniard, too, wore heavy boots—always the symbol to the priest of the invading, grasping, ambitious mind.

The woods, with their grayish, fog-tipped pines, were oppressively silent. It was as if sensing an enemy in the galloping horse and rider, all the living creatures had sought protection in their own immobility. Nothing stirred —not even the leaves of the stubby oaks. Nor did any sound reach the priest from the now not distant village except the occasional high flutelike music he had heard the night before. A thickening feel of death which he had experienced many times before pushed against him from all sides of the woods, and he was pleased to see that where the forest path widened almost to a road, Miguel Viamonte was waiting for him. While greeting the Spaniard again, he reproached himself for his uncharitable thoughts. Somewhere in the man was a quality of godliness—there was in every man. St. Francis would have uncovered it and put it to immediate service. Perhaps today, he told himself, he would discover this quality in Viamonte.

Viamonte, too, had been oppressed by the heavy silence around him, and being a garrulous man, he welcomed the chance to talk—even with the priest whom he found too abstract a speaker for day-by-day conversation.

"You are quite certain a trap is not being prepared for us, padre?" he asked, keeping his horse's pace to that of the priest's unhurried mule.

"Quite certain, of course. Why should the Indians set a trap for an old man and a Spaniard whom they hold in awe?"

"You have confidence in all men, haven't you, Padre Junípero? Even in savages whose ways are unpredictable."

Father Serra's brow creased into deep lines. "It is my nature," he said, "to trust men until they prove themselves untrustworthy. I believe every man merits the opportunity to prove his worth."

"Those are fine words, characteristic of a Latin scholar, but my acquaintanceship has included too many thieves and rogues not to know what fine words actually mean."

"They mean no more than this: when I meet a man, he is good until he proves he is evil."

"And women?"

"It is equally true of women."

"I have never met an honest woman, padre."

"You say a vicious thing, Miguel Viamonte. Have you not a wife in Spain?"

Viamonte pulled the reins of his horse, who was becoming restless with the restraint imposed on him.

"Yes," he said, "you might say I have a wife in Spain."

"It is a pity," the priest said, hoping to direct the conversation away from a discussion of the honesty of women, "that the wives of the colonists do not accompany their husbands. Surely they realize that their place is in the homes the men are building for them."

The Spaniard laughed. "It would require the imagination of a Cervantes or a Lope de Vega to envision my wife at her husband's side in New Spain."

"Why should a woman refuse to share a man's hardships?"

"You do not know women, padre. The only time my wife soils her footwear is when she steps from her carriage to her doorway."

"She could live well in Mexico City. The Spaniards deny themselves nothing there."

"Yes, she could live in greater luxury there than in Aragon, but I have not been able to convince her of this. She believes I invent tales of the luxury of the city only to seduce her."

"Then she must be lonely—waiting for you."

"It is not in my wife's character to be lonely, Padre Junípero. I have been told she has not been lonely since the day I sailed out of the harbor of Cadiz."

"And you, Miguel Viamonte?"

"God help me, I have been. I am. I loved my wife and son. I love them now." His face was flushed from an emotion so close to the surface that Father Serra turned his eyes from the man to the trees still partly hidden by the early-morning mist. Then Viamonte continued: "Those are words I have never said to any man. I have not even whispered them to myself."

"Why do you not return to your family?" the priest asked gently.

"Debts, debts, debts. Why are any of us in New Spain but to escape from debts or from any of the infinite varieties of failure men must escape from? They speak in Spain of the romance and audacity of conquest in faraway lands, but you know as well as I do, Padre Junípero, that these new lands are settled by men of whom it will be said: A few were courageous adventurers, but most of them were weaklings in their own land and scoundrels in a land that was not theirs."

"You are at least honest, Miguel Viamonte."

"No, padre, I am merely honest with you. What can I lose by it—with a priest? I am neither an honest nor a moral man, but I will tell you frankly that I am in New Spain to make a fortune quickly so that I can go home with honor—at least with enough honor to stay out of prison."

"Profits will come slowly to you here. There is no gold in California," the priest said.

"No, that is true, there is no gold in California—but if there were! Imagine, Padre Junípero, if there were, I should be the first white man . . ." The blue of Viamonte's eyes darkened and his hands tightened, then loosened on the reins of his horse. "No," he continued, "there are no great fortunes to be made in California. As soon as we return to Mexico, I shall try to go back to the West Indies."

"The profits in the slave trade satisfy you?"

Viamonte shook his head. "I came too late to enrich myself with the black man. It is too costly, too difficult to obtain them. You see, Cortés and his men were stupidly wasteful of the Cubans, and now the French and the English make it almost impossible for the Spaniards to trade on the other islands."

"Enslavement has never been anything but transitory in the history of the world," Father Serra said. "Slavery is only when a man does not know he is free. It is a thing he learns quickly and then the enslavement is finished. In California, my friend, there will be no slavery, for here men know already they are free. At least they do not know that they are not. It is the same thing."

"In my lifetime and yours, padre, there will be slavery in abundance—perhaps even in California. And I am not concerned with anybody's slave problems of tomorrow."

"Not even with your son's problems?"

"My son will be rich—untouchable," Viamonte said pridefully.

Father Serra shook his head. "Rich, perhaps, but not untouchable. Each generation, fortunately, has its own conflicts to settle. You can give your son gold, but you cannot take him away from his century."

"You speak fine words again, padre, and again I say they have little meaning for me."

"What do you want, Miguel?"

"Gold for tomorrow," Viamonte replied, "and today I want meat, brandy, and a woman."

"You seek only to satisfy the flesh, but surely the demands of the flesh must be more pleasurable when they are subjected to the laws of God," Father Serra said.

"You would have us wait until we returned to our wives, padre?"

"Yes."

"In the meantime we are still men—what would you have us do?"

Father Serra was silent for a moment, and when he spoke it was as if he meant for his words to be heard across the world.

"Love God!" he said.

Miguel Viamonte's face softened into a smile and he almost whispered as he leaned toward the priest.

"You know," he said, "I wonder about Francisco's girl."

He spurred his horse and Father Serra did not see him again until he reached the edge of the village, where Viamonte and Tomás were waiting for him. The fog had completely vanished and the sun was sending whitish rays against the Spaniard's hair and his well-polished boots.

❊   ❊   ❊

The strange trio—the tall, splendid figure on horseback; the priest whose robe almost touched the ground as he sat astride his mule; and the Indian in his homely blue tunic—passed through the village without meeting a single gentile.

As they approached the *himak,* which was the ceremonial enclosure, Father Serra looked up from the dry, sandy road that followed the river bed and watched a solitary figure walking in rhythm with a lethargic drumbeat around the wide top of the wall of the enclosure. In his arms he carried a large pottery jar.

Tomás led the Spaniards into the himak, past two Indians, one of whom was shaking four deer-hoof rattles while the other held a flute in his hands and at long intervals played the mournful, almost terrifying melody Father Serra had heard the night before.

In the center of the enclosure on a pile of rocks surrounded by what seemed to the priest to be every gentile of the village lay an enormous fishing net. Inside the net a frantic eagle struggled to free himself, and while he struggled he screamed. The screams were more like those of a tortured human being than a wounded animal. The gentiles stared soundlessly. The eagle, Tomás whispered to the priest, would be sacrificed to celebrate the proclamation of the new chieftain of the village.

"Where is Boy-Whose-Feet-Are-Wings?" Father Serra asked.

For a moment Tomás hesitated, then guided the priest and the colonist to the farthest end of the enclosure. He stopped beside a deep, sandstone-lined pit, looked into it, then turned away as if sickened by what he saw.

Father Serra stepped past him and when he looked into the pit he quickly made the sign of the cross. "May God help him!" he said.

"Por Diós!" Viamonte cried out. "He needs the help of God indeed."

At the bottom of the pit lay the writhing figure of a man, his hands and feet securely tied with leather thongs. His body was covered with a sticky substance which was being devoured by millions of huge black ants—so thick on his body that it seemed to be encased in a solid black metal garment. By twisting from side to side he could smash the crawling insects but faster than he could kill them they swarmed down the sides of the pit to take the place of the dead and of those which, lethargic from eating, fell from the man's body to the floor of the pit. His face was unrecognizable, his mouth was swollen, and the parts of his body that showed through the sickening mass of greedy insects were red with a mixture of his own blood and that of the dead ants.

"In the name of God," Viamonte whispered. "Those are the stinging ants! I saw them in Cuba. The poor fellow will die." He turned to Tomás. "What crime has he committed that he should merit such punishment?"

In his lifetime Tomás had not witnessed the ordeal of the stinging ants, for it was a torture to which only the contender for the village chiefhood was subjected, and Tomás for the first time was watching the hideous trial of a young potential chieftain. It fascinated him without giving him pleasure, for he knew in his heart that the new God would look upon it with sorrow. From Father Serra's face he knew that.

"From the middle of the night until the middle of the day Boy-Whose-Feet-Are-Wings remains in pit. When the sun stands in the center of the sky, Boy-Whose-Feet-Are-Wings is free. If he is too weak to endure it, he cannot be chief." He looked up at the sun and smiled. "Soon," he said.

Viamonte looked up at the sun, which sent down visible waves of heat upon the village, the himak, the pit, and the agonized body of the boy. He pushed the sweat from his own forehead with his hand and spoke to the priest. "It is your young Indian boy. You are not going to insist upon his release?"

Father Serra shook his head. "This is something they must finish themselves. They must put an end to it only because they know in their hearts that such customs are not the will of God. They still do not know this."

He moved closer to the edge of the pit and called softly to the writhing figure.

A sharp moan came from the boy's lips and he moved his head from one side to the other.

"It is Father Serra, Francisco. Can I help you?"

The boy moved his head again and tried to speak. Crushing the ants around his mouth with his swollen tongue, he formed a word with his lips. It seemed to Father Serra that the boy was asking about the ship.

"No, Francisco," he said, "the ship has not arrived yet,

but have no care. Soon you will see it sail into the harbor."

"Ship," the Indian boy repeated. "Speak to . . . me . . . of . . . the . . . ship."

"It is a great ship with white wings—larger than any ship you have ever seen. The wings are so tall and wide and strong that it can sail for many days and nights upon the water—no matter how evil the waves may be—with the help of God."

"What will the ship bring?" the boy asked.

"It will bring many things; supplies for the men and gifts for your people."

"Gifts?"

"There will be pieces of cloth—heavy white cloth from which Manuel will help you make small wings for your boat. When your boat has wings, you can go far out on the ocean and catch the great fish—perhaps even your enemy, the tuna. There will be beautiful pieces of cloth for dresses—dresses for María and your mother and the other women in the villages. Scissors to cut the cloth and needles and thread to sew it."

"Go on," the boy said.

Father Serra then seated himself close to the pit and waited until the boy had twisted himself into a less torturous position before he continued:

"The ship will bring food: the meat you like and rice and beans, corn meal for tortillas, salt which gives flavor to all foods; seeds to plant in the ground; nails with which to build houses and boats and a school."

"Where does the ship come from?"

The priest talked to the boy of Mexico City and its streets paved with beautiful stones, of its shops and markets. And while the boy listened he talked of Spain and her great cities and of his own island. He described the garments with which men and women clothed their bodies, the ways they had of diverting themselves, the houses they lived in. He spoke of lands he had not seen himself—lands where the sun did not shine and where it rained little drops of white frozen stuff that collected in great drifts and remained on the ground for many days and nights.

He knew that the boy did not want him to stop and, although his mouth was parched and his tongue was swelling from thirst, he talked even when the Indian girl who was to be named María and the boy's mother came to stand beside him. He turned from the boy and looked at the unhappy faces of the women, who could do nothing but wait. And while he talked he prayed to God for patience to bear a little longer with the ignorance that made this suffering necessary. Women, he thought, women are better than men. Women do not torture or torment their fellow beings. It is not women who would capture the great eagle merely to shed its blood. Women do not invent or have any part in torment—they can only stand and watch it, and when the tormented person is one they love, they put themselves in his place, and their suffering is the more devastating. Women do not destroy: they create and protect.

The girl spoke sharply to Tomás, who could not keep his eyes from the sun. Quickly he translated her words for the priest.

"Louder, louder," he said, pointing to his own lips. "If the boy sleeps, he will die."

Father Serra wiped the sweat from his spectacles with his sleeve and looked up at the sun. Red and alive and vicious, it seemed to stand motionless in the sky while it poured its fiercest heat upon the boy in the pit. The boy was twisting his body again and making an effort to form a word with his lips. The word was "St. Francis."

For more than an hour Father Serra spoke of St. Francis —of the boy Francis, handsome son of a rich man, who gave away all his possessions, of the young man Francis who ate from a dish with a leper, of the older man Francis who loved the elements and forgave the element fire for hurting him when a doctor tried to stop his growing blindness by searing his eyeballs.

Watching the boy, the priest knew he must talk, talk, talk. He must shout. He must keep the boy conscious with words. At times he faltered, wondering what had happened to all the words he was master of, what had happened to the eloquence he had learned on Mallorca. At times he talked in a kind of dream, not knowing at all what he was saying. The sun, bigger and bigger, seemed to be filling the whole world with its round red form, and then for Father Serra it lost its form and position in the sky and fell around him and hemmed him in, and he wondered if he could ever make his way through it to the boy. He could no longer hear his own voice, yet sounds were coming from somewhere. And he could see nothing but this peculiar redness and the crawling black forms that grew bigger and bigger until they looked as big as cats. . . .

The sun had reached its highest point and the priest still sat on the ground, forcing words through his blistered lips. In a kind of dream he watched some men lift the boy out of the pit and carry him down toward the river. Then he stretched out on the ground and hid his face from the sun.

It was perhaps an hour later that Father Serra awoke and saw that he had been carried to a covered corner of the himak. When he opened his eyes, Tomás was watching him anxiously.

"Now what?" the priest asked wearily. When Tomás did not reply, he continued: "Now what will happen to Boy-Whose-Feet-Are-Wings?"

"They have bathed him in the river and given him food and drink," Tomás said. "And then . . ." He hesitated and looked down at Father Serra's feet.

"Then?"

"He must fight. He must kill two men."

"The boy must kill two men? Why must he do this?"

"He must kill the two who believe themselves stronger than Boy-Whose-Feet-Are-Wings and desire to be the chieftain."

"The boy would kill two men—two of his own kind?"

"Before the sun dies in the sea. He must."

In spite of his fatigue the priest stumbled to his feet. In addition to torturing himself, Francisco must bear the mark of Cain. Somehow he would have to convince the boy and all his people that only the savage had to destroy the physical man to prove his superiority over him. If only he could speak to these people—simply and eloquently in their own language—he might persuade them. And suddenly he was filled with anger—anger at his own futility, anger at the stupidity of men, anger at the whole race of men who conducted themselves like cruel, unthinking children. Kill, kill —no words of life and love—just hate and kill.

Even the artist, a few yards from where the priest had been lying, protected from the sun, was painting the story of death. His canvas was an enormous stretch of smooth sand, and his tools were a fine-haired brush and some small pottery dishes filled with colors blended from powdered soapstone, charcoal, reddish rust, and a yellowish flower powder. Next to his pictures of the heavens at night and the river and forest and sea by day he was recording the story of the Old Man's death. At this moment he was preparing his colors for the story of the boy and the ordeal of the stinging ants. Many of the gentiles, tired of the struggle of the eagle to free himself, had gathered to watch him. This was their favorite art form. All of them at some time had expressed themselves by painting on the fine, yellow sand.

Father Serra looked at the crowd of people—some of them the women and the men he had baptized and who in a limited way understood what he had tried to teach them. Now, he told himself, now was the time for him to speak. Now was the time for him to say, as God had said thousands of years ago: "Thou shalt not kill!"

Tomás, looking over the priest's shoulder, shouted, "Paint! The padre, too, must paint!"

The people, solemn and expectant, opened a path for the priest, and unsmilingly the artist held out his brush.

Father Serra seized the brush without hesitation. This

was not his medium, but he, too, would paint a story—a story not of death but of life. The most beautiful story men had been privileged to hear.

With awkward but firm strokes of the brush he painted a crude picture of a mule. In it the people recognized Father Serra's mule and for the first time that day they laughed and whispered to each other. The pictures of the man and woman they recognized, too, and again they laughed, for the man wore garments as if he were a woman. They did not understand the smaller figures, which were sheep and lambs, nor the cow, which was quite different from the mule, but they eagerly followed each graceless stroke the priest made with his brush. When he had completed the setting for his story, he began to talk, illustrating his narrative as swiftly and completely as he could. While the story grew, the gentiles gathered in larger numbers, and when he finished Boy-Whose-Feet-Are-Wings had walked back to the himak from the river and was sitting on the ground, his eyes fixed on Father Serra's face and hands.

The story was simple and Tomás explained it to the people in their own language. It told of a father and a mother and a baby who was the Son of God. Of shepherds and angels and wise men who came to worship the child and to bring him gifts. It told the story of a boy who grew to be as strong as Boy-Whose-Feet-Are-Wings—and wise and good as well. And how the boy became a young man and lived near a sea and fished with the fishermen of the village. How when he became a man he was hanged on a cross—not because he was weak or evil, but in order that no other man should have to die, unless he preferred death to life. And how he rose from the tomb to prove that man, too, might be born again. The story of a God who had lived like a man and died like a god—so that men might discover the god in themselves and their own immortality.

It seemed to Father Serra that he had never told the story of life so well as he told it here against the wall of death. It had never been so clear—even to himself; but had they understood anything he had said? He did not know. He did not know how much even Tomás had understood.

When he finished he looked down at Francisco's burned and swollen body.

"God does not ask that man torture himself for God," he said. "Why must man torture himself for man?"

The boy shook his head. "I understand only what my father and his father have told me. Now I must fight. I must kill or be killed."

"As a man of great endurance you can show your people you do not have to kill."

The boy turned his dark, bewildered eyes from the priest to the people, who did not understand what Father Serra was saying to the grandson of the Old Man of the Village. Then he looked again at his friend, the priest.

"To be chieftain, I must kill."

"You have to be chieftain?" Father Serra asked.

The boy was silent for almost a minute. "I am Francisco," he said. "I am the best and the strongest. I will be the chieftain."

Father Serra raised his arms high toward the heavens,

then brought them down hard on the boy's shoulders. His voice was strong, almost menacing.

"Thou shalt not kill!" he said. "Woe to him who dies in mortal sin!"

Without a word the boy rose and moved back through the crowds, and as he walked toward the center of the enclosure where the ground had been smoothed to a hard surface for the fights, the people followed him. . . . Only the priest and the artist remained. The artist had picked up the brush Father Serra had dropped, and was continuing his sketch of the ordeal of the stinging ants.

Father Serra walked toward the open gate of the himak but he could not force himself to leave. Nor could he stand by and watch while a man sought to kill another, not in anger nor in self-defense, but in cool deliberation. He stood near the gate and closed his eyes and prayed.

And while he prayed the boy fought the first challenger. Even with his eyes closed the priest could see the battle . . . the heavy breathing . . . the cries from the spectators . . . their silence . . . the striking of two knives against each other . . . the voice of Viamonte shouting words of encouragement to the boy, "Matale, matale, matale ahora!" Viamonte, a Christian Spaniard, dared urge a man to kill another for no reason . . . no reason. . . . Then the end and Viamonte's words, "Well done, boy. Tu eres muy hombre."

Muy hombre, the priest thought. Very much a man, indeed. He should have wished that it was the boy who was dead—that he had died before he became a murderer . . . a murderer. . . . But he knew in his heart that he did not wish it, even while he watched Viamonte walk with the boy toward his home—to make preparations for his second fight.

Father Serra climbed wearily on his mule to return to the hill and his place by the sea. He could not wait for this other fight, this other murder, though he knew he would have no peace until Viamonte returned to tell him who had survived it. He would not pray for the boy's victory and he could not pray for his death. He knew that if the boy survived and turned to the True God, he would serve his village long and well. He was aware, too, that he wished the boy to live because he loved him as he would have loved his own son.

The Fifth Day

The Fifth Day

D URING THE night Father Serra was not aware of the
change in the sea. On his knees, while he prayed for
the safe arrival of the ship, he let his mind turn for brief
intervals to the disturbing quality of the preceding day, his
physical body unresponsive to the changing pattern of the
waves and winds.

Not until the sky softened and he began to observe the
shapes and sizes of objects about him did he become conscious of the growing violence of the sea. The sea had
whipped itself into a confused mass of waves, which,
catching up the yellow sands, had lost the regularity of
their constant motion toward the shore—had lost even their
sense of direction and were throwing themselves seaward
as well as shoreward. The sea gulls struggled to keep near
the coast line and the shore palms, old to violence and
change, bent with the wind until their tops were on a level
with the salty spray. The wall of fog that usually concealed
the ship from the eyes of anyone on shore had been swept
away by the winds even before the sun rose. Then suddenly Father Serra felt the vicious attack of the elements
around him. It was as if a long-invisible enemy had made
up its mind to come out in open combat.

Shivering while he wrapped his robe closer about his thin body, the priest looked at the possibility of failure— failure in his novena. He looked at it as if it were a dark, shaped thing suspended before his eyes. In his mind was an awareness of some relationship between the success of the novena and his own actions, and when he examined his actions he saw that they were fumbling, awkward, wasteful, lacking in positive achievement. He had converted many of the Indian women and a number of men to his way of worship, yet he had failed, for their conviction had not gone deep enough to meet a crisis like the age-old belief in the moral right of one man to kill another. The Old Man of the Village had died unsaved; one or perhaps two of the young men who had challenged the boy had died in mortal sin; Francisco, who had been his strength in spite of his stubborn opposition to the True God, was a murderer—a twofold murderer—or he was dead. Facing himself here by the menacing sea, Father Serra told himself that he had been given countless opportunities and he had failed. Now he asked himself if he merited the success of his novena, if he deserved new opportunities when he had failed with the old.

Almost immediately he rejected the possibility of failure, dismissing as unworthy of God a relationship between the success of the novena and his own actions. God would not withdraw from this land merely because a weary old man had failed Him. The ship would arrive in time. But time was pressing against him. He had five more days in which to plant God so deep and safe in the hearts of the Indians that the roots would flourish without his care.

While he sat protected from the wind and sticky salt spray by a turn in the cliff, the shadow of a large man approached him on the path leading from the hill. The priest watched eagerly, believing it was Viamonte who had come to bring him news of the village until he saw the dark sober face of the carpenter, Manuel.

"God greet you, Manuel," the priest called out.

"A very good day to you, padre," Manuel replied.

"You have arrived almost before the sun," the priest said. "Is there news?"

Manuel dismissed the question with a shrug of his powerful shoulders. "Father Junípero," he said slowly, "you believe the ship will come." His words were not a question.

"Yes, my son," the priest answered, "the ship will surely come."

"I think I believe it, too."

"You believe it, too?" Father Serra's astonishment showed itself in his voice and on his mood-reflecting face. Although many of the colonists took a desultory part in the priest's daytime prayers, the quality of conviction was missing. The priest was aware of this and daily felt the heaviness of their disbelief, the passiveness of their entreaties.

Manuel spoke laboriously, for tools, not words, were the medium of his expression.

"Perhaps it is only because I wish it so desperately that I believe," he said, "but recently it has seemed to me it must happen, that God in His wisdom will not fail you— even though He may be indifferent to the needs and desires of the rest of us. You see, I have watched you. I watch you each night."

"You watch me?" the priest asked.

Manuel's dark face flushed. "Three of us observe you each night. I watch you during a part of every night."

"But why?"

"Lest some evil happen to you. Let me finish, Padre Serra. What I wish to say is that during these nights the conviction was born in me that the ship will arrive in time."

"It is good of you to say this, Manuel. When I most needed man's consolation, you have brought it to me."

For a moment the carpenter was silent; then he said, "The other two—my companions—we should like to have a more active part in your prayers."

"Who are the other two?"

"Estaban and the little one they call El Gordo. They are both farmers. We—the three of us—should like to join you in your prayers, not only in the chapel but down here by the sea."

A flash of disappointment shot through the priest's feeling of delight in Manuel's words. Down here, alone with God, he was at peace. From now on he must share this place and this time with men. Of course he must. He had prayed that this would happen.

"Yes. It is my only hope. Baja California is desolate. There will never be water for the farms nor green grass for the cattle. The fruits of the earth are indeed meager down there. This, or the more fertile land to the north, is the land I want."

"Then pray, Manuel. Pray as you have not prayed in your life—pray not only with your lips but with your heart and soul and body. Stay on your knees. Live on your knees, Manuel!"

Manuel looked out at the waves that pounded against the shore with the priest's last words as if to give them their own emphasis; then he turned to the hills, which were yellowing again with the rising sun.

"It is a country to dream of, and I am no dreamer," he said. "There is no end to it. In Spain it comes to an end."

"Why did you come to New Spain if you are not a dreamer, not an adventurer, Manuel?"

"It was very simple—as things always are with me. One day I told myself that what I wanted was a piece of ground and a patch of blue sky over it that belonged altogether to me. Two weeks later I sailed out of Cadiz."

"You have done well to come to California, my son. I am certain of it. Spain will prosper on this side of the big continent. Two great nations will lie side by side on this continent, Manuel. Far to the east England lives as New England, and here from the Pacific Spain will continue to extend herself until New Spain will cover more territory than all of Europe. Thousands of Spaniards will come as you have come and for your reasons—and their sons will populate this land. Yes—two great nations will live and grow here—their motherlands occupying only a small portion of Europe."

"Will they live in peace?" Manuel asked.

Father Serra shook his head. "It is not likely—they have never lived in peace in Europe. Still, there is room for all

of them here. Perhaps peace will come with the final set-
tling of boundaries. Peace may come because it is a continent blown clean and fresh by two great oceans."

"And the Indians?"

"They will become a part of each nation. One day there
will be no difference in the blood that flows through the
body of an Indian and that which flows through the white
man's veins."

"England and Spain!" Manuel sighed as he stood up to
go back to the camp. "I should like to see it all. I should
like to see what the Englishmen have achieved on the
Atlantic. Perhaps my children will."

"They accomplish a great deal in spite of the fact that
their climate is not a blessing like ours. There it is cold for
many months—cold as it is in the Pyrenees of Spain, and
one must struggle merely to remain alive."

"Then the civilization of Spain should advance more
quickly than that of England," Manuel said.

"No," the priest said, "it is not in the history of man that
the blessings of climate advance his civilization. No, for
England—on her cold little island—arrived at her age of
gold only a short few years after we achieved our own.
And her greatest poet lived and died along with our own
Cervantes."

Manuel smiled. "I am so ignorant, padre. I did not know
that England had a poet."

"Every country has had a poet, Manuel. A poet is almost
the first thing a country has. Man builds a shelter, he
searches for food and his mate, and then he writes poetry.
That is briefly the history of man."

"The Indians here—they write poetry?"

"They do not write it, they sing it. Yesterday they sang of death."

"What of my young friend, Francisco, padre? Is he now the chieftain of the village?"

"I do not know." The priest looked toward the hill. It was light enough now for him to see the gold baeria and the scarlet bugler that blended together to make a vivid covering for the smooth hill. "Let us go back, Manuel. Perhaps Viamonte has returned from the village with news of Francisco."

* * *

Somewhat to the priest's surprise all his converts among the Indians attended his chapel services that morning, but at the conclusion of the Mass, when he left the chapel to ask them for news of Francisco, they had vanished—even the women who usually lingered to admire the figure of the Child Jesus.

He walked over to his own camp and was eating his breakfast atole when he heard the voices of Comandante Portolá and Viamonte not far from his door. He rose to speak with them, then changed his mind and sat down to finish his breakfast.

"You had a difficult night, Viamonte?" The comandante's voice shook with amusement. "You are in desperate need of repair and sleep."

"Father Serra's savages are indeed savages," Viamonte said angrily. "They will always be savages. I tell you, comandante, I will be the first man aboard the ship when we sail for Mexico."

"When the padre last saw you, he told me, you were acting as Francisco's second in a fight to the death. What happened to the boy?"

"I won his fight for him—his second fight. His condition is not good, but he lives."

"You won his fight?"

"With my good advice, comandante. His first fight and his ordeal with the stinging ants had exhausted him, and I instructed him how to win the second battle. Instead of the prolonged demonstration of skill with the knife—not unlike the duel for a woman's honor in Spain with swords —I showed him how to trick his opponent—how to bring his knife up sharply into the bowels of the other man while he did not expect it. This the boy did and with such skill that nobody saw it happen. They saw only the blood and the intestines of the man who had been killed and who fell over with a look of pained surprise that would have made you laugh."

"I do not know why you wished to help the boy. I thought you disliked him."

"I did. I do. But there was something about the way he endured the ordeal of the stinging ants that moved me— that put me on his side. I wanted him to win his fights. Jesucristo, Comandante, if you had seen those crawling things . . ."

"And after the fight?" Gaspar de Portolá, who never looked into the eyes of the man he talked with, watched a lizard move rapidly to a sunny spot on the wall.

"The Indians, damn them, thought that the fight was a miracle, a miracle of the white man's god—and before I could get out of the enclosure the young men had surrounded me and began to sing and scream—which, with them, is the same thing. The Man-Whose-Hair-Is-the-Sun is the white man's god!"

The comandante roared with laughter and slapped his friend hard on the back.

"A fine joke," he said.

"Yes. At first it diverted me. They fed me some of the food they had prepared to bury with the ashes of the Old Man, and they brought me pitchers of some kind of drink —not a bad drink at all, though it had the flavor of the acorn that seems to be their only food. Acorns and stinking rotten fish, por Dios!"

"Did they expect more miracles of you, Señor Viamonte?"

"I suppose they did, but I disappointed them. I soon wearied of the demonstration—I have not the physical endurance to be a god—but I could not get away. For an hour in the hot sun and for an hour after sunset I was given the position of honor on the wall of death."

"The wall of death?"

"Yes, they demanded that I march around the top of the wall with the pottery jar that contained the Old Man's ashes."

Portolá laughed again. "It was an honor I do not begrudge you, Viamonte."

"It was an honor I protested to no avail. In fact I was fortunate that they allowed me to come down after two hours. Some poor devil has the honor of marching around that wall for six days and nights!"

"But how did you pass the night, or is that something you wish to confess only to the padre? I must say that, although you look weary, you do not have the appearance of a satisfied man."

Viamonte frowned, then continued:

"There was an enormous supper with more of the acorn pancakes and fish and the fermented drink that affected me at first like brandy, then made me vomit. You doubtless heard the music—if you are willing to call it music. That accompanied the dancing, which did not stop, I promise you, until the sun rose."

"Why did you not return to the camp?"

"I tell you, it was not possible. I was surrounded by Indians who danced with their bows and arrows in their hands."

"Yet they are friendly."

"I was not—I am not—certain of that. They danced before me as if they were performing for a great king, and yet I was not certain they were not mocking me. I was indeed uncomfortable. Besides—there were the women."

"Oh, yes," the comandante said, "what about the women? Did they offer you one? Surely the white man's god merited a woman."

Viamonte's voice lowered and was scarcely audible even to the comandante.

"There was only one I desired, and although she came close to me many times while she danced, I was unable to seize her."

"That is unlike you, Viamonte. Of course it was Francisco's promised bride?"

Viamonte ran his tongue over his dry lips.

"Her sister—the loca—danced close to me and even reached out to touch me, while Francisco's girl followed her—never more than a yard away." Viamonte was whispering now. "One time Francisco's girl came so near I was able to touch her, but before I could put my arm around her she had slipped away. God in heaven, comandante, I have never seen people who could vanish like witches." Again he moistened his lips. "Nor have I ever seen such breasts. If I have I have forgotten whose or where or when."

The comandante yawned. "You speak like a soldier in his first year, Viamonte. Why did you not find the girl and have her?"

Viamonte was not listening. "You know, comandante, I should even be willing to marry an Indian like that one."

The comandante stared at his friend. "Marry her? You have a wife in Spain, remember?"

The colonist was still speaking softly. "I also have a wife in Cuba."

"You are mad, Viamonte, to think you could or would marry that girl."

"Oh, no, I do not think I would. I merely said I should be willing to. I should like to be married to a woman who would look at me as that girl looks at her Indian—with warmth and tenderness."

"You are a fool, Viamonte. Now it will be best for you to see to your own affairs up here and make preparations for our return to Mexico. There's a lot of work to be done, and I have promised the padre that the chapel will be finished before we leave the post for Mexico."

"The sea is high today," Viamonte said. "The sea is high and rough and only a man is strong enough to dominate it, enslave it. Only the sea is worthy of man's domination. To conquer men is scarcely worth the trouble."

"What are you talking about, Viamonte?" Portolá asked sharply.

"The sea, comandante," Viamonte replied.

❋　　❋　　❋

In the afternoon Francisco's two young companions appeared in the stockade, indicating with their hands that they wished to carry logs for the chapel; four or five of the Indians who had attended the morning services stayed to work under Villalobos' direction; the Spaniards who had been restless and vigilant for the past two days relaxed and went about their daily chores. Except for the occasional shrill singing that came out of the Indian village and the absence of Francisco the day was much like the other days.

Not until late in the afternoon did Father Serra walk back down to the sea. After he had spoken with Viamonte about Francisco he had been busy with his visits to the men in the hospital camp and later he had sat at the little table in his own camp and outlined plans for the big fiesta that would follow the arrival of the ship.

Still thinking of the ceremony of the hanging of the

chapel bells in which the Indian children were to take important parts, he hobbled down to his place by the cliffs for a short rest before the evening services.

Francisco was waiting for him as if he had known the priest would come down at this hour. Father Serra looked at the boy gravely. His body was still swollen with red, ugly sores, and a long knife wound cut across his chest from his shoulder to his waist. He was holding firmly to something in his hand.

"I came to see my boat and to bring you a gift," the boy said.

The priest did not reply. Francisco, he thought sorrowfully, was no longer a boy and not quite a man. The boy in him spoke eagerly of a boat, of a gift; the man in him had taken on a kind of dignity in the place of his young arrogance. Young enough to play with a boat, old enough to rule a village, he stood in front of the priest uncertain of his friend's feelings toward him.

The priest looked at the wound on the boy's chest and thought of the scars on his own body—scars he had inflicted upon himself with a whip. He had beaten his own body out of love for God and dissatisfaction with his own shortcomings. This wound on Francisco's body was the result of a kind of flagellation, too, but it was not proof of his love of God; it was the symbol of man's vanity and ignorance and belief in his own strength and invincibility.

When the priest remained silent, the boy spoke again:

"Padre, when a white man does an evil thing and wishes he had not done it, what does he then say?"

"He gets down on his knees to his God and says, 'Father,

I have sinned grievously. Punish me and forgive me. I will try to sin no more.' "

"I have done no evil thing," the boy said. "Yet when I looked down upon the dead bodies of my friends I wished I had not killed them. It is not easy to kill a friend even when it is the law of the village."

"The law of God surpasses the law of a village," the priest said. "Francisco, you have sinned, you have done an evil thing. In your heart you know this—otherwise you would not be unhappy today."

Francisco knelt at his friend's feet and looked into his dark, serious eyes.

"Yet you will forgive me, will you not, padre?"

The priest stretched out his hand and placed it on the boy's shoulder. He would have liked to say, "Go see about your boat, my son. Everything is well." Instead, he spoke sternly: "When you have confessed your sins and are prepared to repent, you will be forgiven."

"Then you are no longer my friend?" Francisco asked.

"I am indeed your friend," Father Serra replied. "I pray each day for your salvation."

The boy smiled. "Then you will take my gift," he said. He opened his hand and showed Father Serra a small crude cross he had made from a piece of wild walnut.

"This is to take the place of the cross you left to be buried with the Old Man," he said. He looked at it proudly. "It is a very fine cross," he said. "It is perhaps better than the one you gave the Old Man?" he asked, looking anxiously at the priest.

Father Serra smiled. "It is a good cross," he said. And

while he searched in his mind for the right words to say to Francisco, he heard a scream, a loud scream that sent the sea gulls far out on the rising sea.

❀   ❀   ❀

That afternoon Miguel Viamonte rose from his siesta, hot and irritable and bored. He had crippled his horse in the ride from the village, and now there was nothing to occupy his time. For about a half hour he worked on his boots, polishing them, then polishing them again. Finally he got up in disgust and decided to go swimming in the sea. That would at least cool off his body. He started down the hill, then changed his course toward the sea beyond the cliff. He was in no mood to have words with a priest, and the priest was no doubt on his knees in his customary place near the shore line.

There was no path to the sea from this approach, and he was cursing his ill luck when he looked down toward the water and saw the figure of a girl. He did not recognize her but he walked faster for fear she would vanish—as these damned Indians had the habit of vanishing. Then again he cursed his bad luck. The girl was the mad one, the loca, whom Father Serra had baptised Cecilia.

The girl was alone, and when she saw Miguel Viamonte she stared for a moment, then smiled. There was no meaning in her smooth face and no expression in her eyes. She did not move when the big Spaniard stopped beside her.

"White god," she whispered, still smiling.

Viamonte walked on toward the cliff, then turned

around. The girl was watching him, her hands clasped tight against her breast. Except for the stupid look on her face she was not unlike the little one, María. He walked slowly back to the girl and spoke softly.

"Come with the white god," he said. "Come and see where the white god lives."

As if she had understood his words she followed him toward the cliff and into a small cavelike recess where he usually left his clothes when he swam in the sea.

Gently he placed a hand on her hair and on her cheek, and when he saw that she was not frightened he led her to the back of the cave and sat down beside her. She reached over to touch his hair and he pulled her into his arms.

Quickly he removed her bodice and her skirt while she lay there without protest. If he had looked at her he would have seen the fear tightening across her smooth dark forehead. Then he threw himself upon her body and she screamed. He struck her across the face and she screamed again. In the cave it sounded loud enough to be heard as far as the Indian village. Viamonte thought of the priest, who could be no more than a few yards away on the other side of the cliff, and while he hesitated, the girl forced herself out of his hands and ran naked out of the cave down to the sea. Viamonte ran toward her and when she turned and saw him she screamed again. It was this scream that had alarmed the sea gulls.

Francisco caught sight of Viamonte before he saw the girl, who had already reached the shallow waters of the sea and was still running seaward. When he recognized the girl he called to her to stop, then ran and plunged into the waves.

Father Serra waited. The time was as endless as it had been the day before when the sun stopped in the heavens. Actually it was about fifteen minutes before he saw Francisco swimming toward the shore with the body of the girl.

When Francisco reached the shallow water, he picked the girl up in his arms and stood for a moment looking from one direction to the other like a panic-stricken animal from the forest. Then carrying the girl's body as if it had no weight he ran toward the village by the long route that kept him out of the sight of the Spaniards on the hill.

Father Serra, who had not taken his eyes from the sea, glanced toward the cliff. Viamonte had disappeared. . . . It was not until the middle of the night when he heard the wailing songs and saw the reflection in the sky of the village fires that the priest could believe the girl he had named Cecilia was dead.

The Sixth Day

The Sixth Day

AFTER A night of prayer—this time in the company of three men—Father Serra got off his knees and faced the day with an almost certain knowledge of coming disaster.

During the night he had pondered in his self-examining way on the events of the day, contrasting his failure here to his success in northern Mexico. There, of course, he had not asked God to limit Himself in time. There where time had moved on unmarked except by holydays, Junípero Serra had spent the first weeks learning the Pamé dialect. Then he had preached to the people. It had not been easy for the simple Indians to resist the Franciscan's impassioned oratory—coupled as it was with his unquestionable affection for the Indians. Later he had written a simple catechism and some of the prayers in the Pamé language and had taught the Indians to sing. Those who had been able to resist his theology and his not altogether tuneful singing had been attracted to the Church by the holyday rituals, which he made simple but dramatic and in which the Indians played the major roles. To Father Serra, his own aesthetic feelings lost in his appreciation of simple belief, the primitive, naïve performances had been quite moving and beautiful. To him the adoration of the small Indian baby in the Nativity ritual had not been unlike his

157

own conception of the worship of the Child Jesus Himself. The Church had not been his only gift to the Indians of Mexico. The son of a hard-working farmer, Junípero Serra had learned the rudiments of farming during his young years and had brought his knowledge to people who had desperate need of it. There had been no doubt of its success. The Indians who lived in the mission lived better than they had lived in the wilderness and they lived longer. Although a few had abandoned the mission for their old savage life, most of them had returned, and the process of conversion had moved steadily forward. Even after Father Serra's return to Mexico City, the seed he had planted in the wilderness had flourished.

But in addition to rain and sun and fertility and care, seed needed time. Never had the priest felt the need for unlimited time as he felt it on this morning of his sixth day—the sixth day of his prayer for the shortening of his time among the San Diego Indians. While his soul pleaded for the arrival of the ship that would carry him away, his heart and mind were concerned with the need for his stay here. The conflict exhausted him and he walked up the hill with no feeling of refreshment from a night of prayer by the sea.

He was tormented, too, by his thoughts of the girl Cecilia, the girl who in the woods had saved his life. If she was dead—and the sounds from the village made him certain she was—his small achievement among her people would be completely undone. They had looked upon the poor, demented girl as one protected by a spirit which was not here but which belonged to someone who had lived before, and they had lived in some awe of her confusion, attributing it to the fact of the two spirits that lived in her. Unlike the foolish and imbecilic of other lands, she had lived secure and beloved among her people. A white man had driven her to sea which was synonymous with death. Only death inhabited the sea. No word or act of a priest could bring life where death was.

Father Serra's feeling of pity and sorrow vanished into sudden anger when he thought of the reason for the girl's death—the stupid, vicious reason. Miguel Viamonte was one of those men who walked heavily across the earth, leaving no marks but those of violence and hatred. Some men walked heavily out of clumsiness and thoughtlessness, but men like Viamonte left their deep, ineradicable traces out of viciousness. Those men of good will—like Manuel Villalobos, who had helped the Indian boy with the boat—walked lightly upon the earth and into the hearts of other men. Father Serra wondered if such men left a trace at all. If the Church had to be abandoned in this wilderness, which memory of the white man would remain? The memory of a man who helped build a boat or the memory of a man who drove a girl into the sea? Further angered by the answer to this question, which he knew well, the priest hurried to the top of the hill, taking no thought of his bad leg. Not for many days did he remember that no one who had walked across the earth and into the hearts of men had walked so softly as St. Francis and that his God, who had walked upon the earth as a man, had walked lightly enough to tread the surface of the sea.

He put off seeing the Spaniard Viamonte until after the morning services in the chapel, but the anger stayed in his heart. When he observed that of all the gentiles who had been converted only Tomás attended the morning Mass, his anger toward the Spaniard broke into his usual continuity of feeling and thought, destroying the serenely reverent mood that was characteristic of all his chapel services. He did not even notice that for the first time the Indian Tomás came to the chapel armed with his bow and arrows.

Gaspar de Portolá waited for Father Serra at the sacristy door, and after an abrupt greeting, he looked across the churchyard, his small eyes searching for something that was not there.

"You believe, padre, that the absence of the gentiles this morning can be laid to Viamonte's indiscretion of last evening?" he asked.

Father Serra held up his hands as if he might thrust from him the frivolous, offensive attitude of the comandante, who believed that the colonist's behavior was no more than an indiscretion. Then he pushed back his spectacles and stared at the officer.

"Viamonte," he said finally, "is a murderer. What steps have you taken for his punishment?"

The comandante stopped looking for the invisible object and turned to see if the priest was joking—unlikely as it was.

"Viamonte is no murderer," he said. "Have you been informed that the girl is dead?"

"You know it as well as I do," the priest replied. "You

heard the sounds and you saw the flames. And you did not
hear the singing voice which was Cecilia's. May she rest
in peace. I know she died."

"Viamonte told me what happened. The girl followed
him, tormented him, and he did what any man would do
—he undressed her, made love to her."

"And drove her to the sea."

"The girl was an idiot. You know that. For some insane
reason she flung herself into the sea. Viamonte did not
murder her."

"Then why do you ask about the gentiles, comandante?
Why are you concerned with their absence from the
morning service?"

"Because I do not trust them. Because, like Indians
everywhere, they would not hesitate to use that girl's
death as an excuse to drive us from the harbor. I worry
about their silence this morning."

"They mourn for a girl who to them was more than a
human being like themselves. They believe that two spirits
lived in her body—that one of them dwelt in her throat
and gave her the power to sing as they had never heard
anyone sing before. She sang of things they knew well and
of things they did not understand at all—it was she who
sang of the white god and it was she who believed Viamonte was the white man's god. She came here—with all
her fear—to worship him. She came to sing her song.
Viamonte silenced the song."

The comandante walked restlessly from one end of the
shaded patch in front of the chapel to the other.

"Viamonte behaved like a fool, I must admit," he said.

"And he will be punished. You may tell them that. The Indian Tomás is here—he can deliver your message to his people."

"First I will speak with Miguel Viamonte," the priest said. "I will speak with him now."

The comandante hesitated for a moment. "I am afraid you will find him quite unrepentant, Father Serra."

Father Serra's hands trembled from the anger that shook his whole body.

"Viamonte sinned before God. He shall repent before God! And it is your duty to place him where he can do no further harm to the cause of God and Spain."

"You are speaking of me and my sins?" a soft voice asked. Miguel Viamonte, clean and glittering from a swim in the sea, had come up behind the priest from the brow of the hill. "Before breakfast?"

The comandante, who had no patience with men who lusted after women to the peril of his camp, greeted Viamonte curtly and walked away in the direction of the camp kitchen.

"The comandante is angry this morning," the colonist said. "He did not sleep last night. In spite of his two cannons, which could destroy the whole village of Indians, he fears for his skin."

"And you, Viamonte," the priest said, "do you not fear for your immortal soul?"

"Padre Junípero," Viamonte said, "I am bored with the whole subject of an imbecile girl who threw herself into my arms. I did not even desire her."

The priest, whose voice a moment before had spread

through the courtyard reaching the ears of every man who listened, was now low, almost inaudible.

"A girl whose presence in her village had the deepest significance is driven into the sea, and Miguel Viamonte is bored," he said. "A whole village of people—people with blood in their veins and hearts in their bosoms—mourn for their beloved, but Miguel Viamonte is bored. An entire village of pagans may be lost to God forever, but Miguel Viamonte is bored. A girl too weak and full of trust to defend herself is raped and slain, but Miguel Viamonte is bored. A man breaks two of God's commandments and he is bored. He yawns. He does not trouble himself to conceal his yawn."

The priest's voice rose. He walked up two of the chapel steps and looked down upon the astonished Spaniard.

"Miguel Viamonte," the priest continued, "your God through your priest calls upon you to repent—to confess your sins and to do penance. Woe to him who knows his sin and does not confess it. Woe to him who does not fall upon his knees and beg God to forgive him. Woe to you, Miguel Viamonte, who on this day and in this spot do not cleanse yourself of your crime against God and one of his weakest creatures!"

Viamonte trembled and looked as if he might fall upon his knees that minute and in that place. Then he heard the voices of the soldiers and colonists who had moved nearer to listen to their priest's menacing words. Flushing with embarrassment and anger, Viamonte pushed his way through the groups of men and hurried to the camp kitchen. Father Serra watched him disappear before he limped back into the chapel. The men, restrained to silence for the moment by the priest's anger and Viamonte's insolence, whispered among themselves, then laughed and shouted and went back to their affairs. Such moments released them from their daily stupefying boredom.

* * *

A few minutes before the midday meal, Father Serra heard sounds of laughter from a large group of soldiers. Not since he had left Mexico had he heard anyone laugh out of pure enjoyment, and the sound comforted him. He walked toward the stables, where the men had formed a deep circle around something and were laughing and shouting and hitting each other on the back.

When he reached the edge of the circle one of the soldiers called out, "You know, Padre Junípero, the comandante has a baby!"

The circle opened for the priest and when he got well inside the stable he saw what was amusing the soldiers. The comandante's mare had given birth to a small black colt. Sucking greedily at her mother's teats, the little animal seemed to be nothing but four long, slim, shining black legs. The camp surgeon, who had taken over the duties of the camp veterinarian now sick in the hospital, was kneeling beside the mare. The comandante, red and sweating, knelt beside him.

"How is the mare, Don Pedro?" he asked anxiously.

"She will be fine now, comandante," the doctor said.

"For an hour I was not certain. This is the first four-legged female whose birth I have attended."

"Look!" one of the soldiers cried out. "She is nothing but legs!"

"What else do you want . . . on a woman?" someone asked.

The soldiers pushed against each other to get closer to the colt, all talking at the same time.

The Indian Tomás stood at Father Serra's side. His dark eyes opened wide at the sight of the colt and he moved quietly forward to lay his hand on the animal's back. When the mare whinnied, he jumped back, frightened. The men laughed. The comandante looked at the Indian and then at Father Serra.

"It is possible," he said, "that I will not keep the colt. Perhaps I should give it to the village, to the boy Francisco. Where is Francisco?"

"In the village," the priest answered. "But that is a worthy idea."

"What about you, Tomás?" the comandante said. "Perhaps you want a colt? She will grow to be large like her mother."

Tomás could not believe what the comandante was saying and he turned to the priest for an explanation.

"The comandante would give you the colt," the priest said slowly. "To you, Tomás."

Tomás stared at the comandante and then got down on his knees beside the colt. "Little horse," he whispered, "for Tomás." He touched the colt's head and when the mare whinnied again he did not jerk his hand away. Instead, he caressed the mare's head gently and then he spoke to the comandante. "You do not tell me a lie?"

The comandante laughed. "No, Tomás. I will give you the little horse. It is a gift for the village, but she will be your responsibility. You will take care of her."

"You are all idiots," the doctor interrupted. "How will the colt be fed? You cannot take her from her mother's milk for several weeks."

"I am stupid, doctor," the comandante said. "Of course she must stay with her mother. And in a few days we shall return to Mexico." He did not want to look at Tomás' worried eyes. "Explain the laws of nature to Tomás, padre," he said.

For several minutes Tomás and the priest whispered together, each trying to make the other understand his language. Then the priest spoke to the comandante.

"Tomás believes he can feed the colt. He can keep her supplied with the milk of the coconut that grows farther up the coast."

The comandante was thoughtful. He would like to give the colt to the Indian, yet the animal had value. He would rather lose a man than a good beast.

"What is your opinion, doctor?" he asked.

The doctor shrugged his shoulders. "I have seen it done for a mule. I cannot answer for a horse."

Again Tomás was on his knees by the colt, his solemn eyes fixed on the comandante's face.

"Very well, Tomás. The little horse is yours," the comandante said finally. "You will take good care of her. If you let her die I will come back and cut your ears off."

"She will not die," Tomás said. "I promise. She will live to be as old as the Old Man of the Village. I take her now." He leaned over as if to pick the colt up in his arms.

"No," the comandante said. "She is yours, but she must stay with her mother until we leave the harbor."

"You leave soon?" the Indian asked hopefully.

"In three days," the comandante said.

Tomás stooped to rub his dark hand against the colt's neck and to touch the tiny white star above her eyes. Then with no more words he ran through the circle of men out of the enclosure, and down the hill toward the village.

Father Serra broke into the silence that had suddenly encompassed the camp.

"It was a good thing—a kind thing to do, comandante," he said.

"At least an intelligent thing, padre," the comandante said. "We owe them something. The horse is little enough to offer them for . . ." He looked down at the colt, who for a moment had stopped tugging at her mother's teats. "She is indeed a pretty one, is she not, padre?" he said, "and of excellent appetite."

❀   ❀   ❀

One could in no way predict the behavior of the Indian. Father Serra had told himself this ever since he reached the New World, and he thought of it again as he looked over his congregation at the evening service and saw that all his gentiles, the men and women and the children over five years of age, were kneeling on the chapel floor. The men—almost all of them—were wearing loincloths fashioned from bits of cloth they had begged or perhaps stolen from the Spaniards. He had supposed they would continue to absent themselves from the chapel until judgment had been passed on the death of Cecilia, but they were here before him. God in His wisdom had given him another opportunity.

Lighted by a single candle—his last one—and solemnized by the repeated discharges of the soldiers' muskets—the only incense left him—the evening service continued long after sunset.

Father Serra could not let the people go, for it seemed to him that as long as he held them in the chapel no evil could come to them or through them. At first he had thought to move them by threats of eternal punishment. He had even considered showing them the contempt he had for the earthly body by beating his shoulders with a heavy chain as he had done frequently in Mexico City when he felt tormented by the comfort-loving, privilege-crazy Spaniards. But to do this he needed anger, and his anger of the morning had vanished. Thinking of the people before him—Indians and Spaniards—he felt nothing but pity and a deep, unquestioning love.

In the middle of the informal service, which he always adapted to suit the needs and moods of the moment, he allowed them to sing a song he had taught them in Spanish. It was nothing but a loud, disorderly cacophony, but to the priest it was not at all unpleasant and for the Indians it was an exciting expression of their feelings.

Toward the end of the service Father Serra talked to them again of St. Francis, and instead of his usual Latin prayers he recited for them the saint's *Canticle of the Sun* which Francisco had helped him translate into their language. These were words he was certain they would understand. He himself understood them very well indeed.

"Praised be the Lord God with all His creatures, and especially our brother the sun who brings us the day and who brings us the light; fair is he and shines with a very great splendor.

"Praised be the Lord God for our sister the moon, and for the stars, the which he has set clear and lovely in heaven.

"Praised be the Lord God for our brother the wind, and for air and cloud, calms and all weather by which Thou upholdest life in all creatures.

"Praised be the Lord God for our sister water, who is very serviceable unto us and humble and precious and clean.

"Praised be the Lord for our brother fire, through whom Thou givest us light in the darkness, and he is bright and pleasant and very mighty and strong.

"Praised be the Lord for our mother the earth, who bringeth forth diverse fruits and flowers and grass of many colors.

"Praised be the Lord for our sister the death of the body, from which no man escapeth. Woe to him who dieth in mortal sin!"

Repeating the final sentence in a voice that had changed from one of exuberance to one of ominous prophecy, he searched among his congregation for the face of Miguel Viamonte, but Viamonte was not in the chapel.

After he had changed his vestments he left the sacristy to speak with the gentiles but when he walked to the front of the chapel the Indians had disappeared. Puzzled again by their behavior, he stood on the chapel steps and listened for some sound of them in the dark, starless night. Finally he saw them, massed like an army near the gate of the stockade. Chuckling to himself he walked toward them. But once more his vanity had tricked him. He had believed the Indians had come to the stockade this night to listen to his fine words. They had not. They had come to see the little horse. They were waiting their turn at the door of the stable.

* * *

In the middle of the night Gaspar de Portolá interrupted the nightlong prayers of Father Serra and his three companions. He did not want to alarm the camp but not since late afternoon had Viamonte been seen. He would not have ridden to the village—even Viamonte did not have such courage—but he was not in the stockade. The comandante was worried.

Father Serra was immediately alarmed. Earlier in the day a certain knowledge had beaten inside his brain—the knowledge that the death of Cecilia would not be passively accepted by Francisco, now chief of the village. But he had forgotten it—at first in his pleasure with the chapel service, later in the urgency of his prayers for the arrival of the *San Antonio*. Now he remembered the look on Francisco's face when the boy had caught a glimpse of Viamonte and had then plunged into the sea to bring back the naked body of Cecilia. Before the sun had died again in the sea, Francisco would have surely avenged her—or he would have made a courageous attempt.

What was the punishment for rape and murder among the San Diego Indians? Francisco had told the priest on his first visit to the village, but he did not remember. That the punishment was not death, he was certain. It was a torture. He thought of the ordeal of stinging ants and shuddered, but that was the trial of a hero, not a punishment for the wickedly lustful.

"Have you searched the cave?" the corporal asked. "Viamonte often slept in the cave after his bath in the sea."

With the aid of a heavy stick Father Serra hobbled along behind the four men. The cave was about half a mile from Father Serra's place of rest and prayer, but the night was so dark and the sea beat so violently against the rocks, that he lost them several times. Each time they waited for him patiently—as if when they found the colonist they wanted the priest to be with them.

While he stumbled along the wet sands he prayed. He prayed that Viamonte would be alive, that the boy Francisco would not carry the burden of a third murder. He prayed that Viamonte would not have died unconfessed and in mortal sin. "God have mercy on both their souls," he whispered. "God have mercy on the whole race of man who kill and must kill again."

The cave was dark but the sounds of the sea were muffled and the men for the first time could hear their own voices. The comandante carried a torch and when he had finally succeeded in setting it afire he held it high in the air, so that gradually the light filled the cave.

It was Manuel who first saw Viamonte. He was lying on the ground with his feet and hands bound with thongs—as Francisco had lain in the pit. His clothes had been removed and thrown aside. There was nothing else in the cave. Cecilia's garments had been taken away.

When the comandante brought the torch and held it over Viamonte, the Spaniards saw the punishment—the Indians' punishment for rape and murder. The man was not dead, but he was unconscious from unendurable pain. Across his chest from his waist to his shoulders was a gigantic red symbol which looked like a huge letter "S" with lines perpendicular to the top and the bottom. It looked as if it had been painted on his body with some sticky, red-colored substance, but the substance was not paint. The symbol had been cut out of Viamonte's flesh. Even now the blood was not quite dry.

Then Father Serra remembered. The symbol cut from a man's flesh, leaving a permanent scar on his chest, was the Indians' mark for their Cains.

When the four men had carried Viamonte out of the cave, the priest returned to his place by the sea. There was nothing he could do for the Spaniard's body, but he could pray for his soul.

The Seventh Day

The Seventh Day

W AS St. Francis so at one with the elements and
their Creator that even the winds turned, matching
their rhythm and direction with his? Father Serra asked
himself that question as he stood on the beach while the
winds of the rising storm whipped around his body and
all but sent him sprawling upon the sands. He remembered
that the mountain wolves as well as the birds and insects
felt no enmity in the first Franciscan, and now he asked
himself if the beloved and loving saint was so at one with
the universe that all its creatures moved without question
in the direction he chose. On the other hand, was he,
Junípero Serra, so out of harmony with the same universe
that he must constantly move contrariwise to its elements
as well as to its creatures? Then he questioned himself
further. What was this harmony and how had St. Francis
achieved it? It was, yes, it must be love—the kind of love
God spoke of—love that casts out fear in oneself and in the
object beloved. That was what St. Francis had achieved
and what Junípero Serra had failed to achieve: perfect
love, unlimited in its capacity—hence an infinite harmony
with the world in contrast to the finite harmony of his,
Father Serra's.

The morning, blackened into near-evening by the coming storm, wrapped its salty mists around him, and in spite of his heavy cloak the priest shivered. Yet he did not want to leave his haven. It was as if by staying here he could hold the day back—the day and the evils that would come out of it.

He watched the crash and hurl of the waves while they —deliberate, insolent, menacing—heaved themselves upon the shore, then heaved themselves again, each time measuring their force, then redoubling it.

A ship, especially one not acquainted with these waters, would have trouble making its way into the port. Like himself, the priest thought, the ship was perhaps riding in a whirlwind out of step with the sea. But with the help of God, who directed the storms and calmed the whirlwinds, the *San Antonio* would reach the port safely. This the priest knew. Whatever else happened, the *San Antonio* would arrive before the end of the ninth day. Beneath the wind-maddened surface the sea was deep and quiet, and in a few minutes the wild surface could be conquered—if it were the will of God.

Then he turned from the sea and prepared to climb the hill, abandoning his thoughts of the sea and the ship to clear his mind for the work of the day. Viamonte would be in his camp, suffering from the wounds of the Indian's knife. The Indians had their revenge; he hoped Miguel Viamonte would consider the affair settled. Surely he would realize that the punishment for his kind of sin was merciful enough. Yet it was true that when men took revenge out of God's hands there was often no end to it. Such a thing here could lead to a gigantic, unending feud between the white men and the Indians and any hope of a chain of great, peaceful missions in New California would have to be given up—given up for men's pride and men's lust. In some way he must put an immediate end to this feud . . .

But even while he promised himself this, the storm in the hearts of the men now close to him raged, the waves of hatred crashing and hurling themselves—measuring their force, then redoubling it, to crash and hurl again. . . . Father Serra did not know this until later in the day.

He felt at his ease during the morning Mass, for as on the evening before all his gentiles were in attendance. That afterward they again went directly to the stables and crowded around the mare with her colt amused him, and he asked the camp cook to prepare a huge pot of atole for them from the fast-disappearing store of corn meal. While they ate the steaming bowls of mush, he asked them about Francisco. The boy was now chief of the village, Tomás explained, and very busy. Soon he would marry. For fifteen settings of the sun after the wedding he must leave the village with his bride, or his brides if he married the two sisters. In the meantime he had many things to do. He had asked Tomás to make his boat secure against the rising storm.

After breakfast Father Serra filled a pottery jar with the herb poultice he used on his bad leg and walked across the stockade to the camp hospital.

To his surprise Miguel Viamonte greeted him in a friendly manner and even allowed the priest to spread the evil-smelling poultice over the wounds of his chest. He agreed, too, that he should expose his chest to the healing properties of the sun. Unfortunately, he added, the sun had decided to conceal itself today.

Father Serra wondered at the man's good spirits after a night of intense suffering, but as was his custom when confronted by a positive attitude in a man, he did not examine it too closely. He accepted Viamonte's response as the response of a man chastened and perhaps repentant. The conflict had doubtless spent itself . . . like a great wave receding from a rock, weakening until it was only an infinitesimal part of the ocean itself.

Nevertheless, he felt compelled to put some of his thoughts and feelings into words.

"It pleases me," he said, "to see that you are recovering quickly from your misadventure."

"Yes," said Viamonte, "the wounds will doubtless heal themselves quickly."

"It pleases me, moreover," the priest continued, "to observe that you carry no ill will in your heart."

"No, I carry no ill will," the Spaniard said. His face was white from the loss of blood, but his voice was strong.

"Then may God bless you," said Father Serra, "and forgive your sins as you forgive those who injured you. The Indians erred out of ignorance and punished you according to their own tradition, not according to the will of God or the laws of white men. Let this evil thing—revenge—stop now, Miguel Viamonte."

"I am indeed satisfied, padre," Viamonte said softly. "I hope you can persuade the Indian people to be as satisfied as I am."

"It was Francisco, was it not, Viamonte?"

"Yes, it was Francisco."

Father Serra felt a stirring of discomfort which he invariably felt when he spoke with Miguel Viamonte. It was always as if the words spoken stood between them, as if they had nothing to do with the man who spoke them or the man who listened to them, but were merely used to fill up the silence between the two men. The feeling remained with him as he left the camp hospital and went in search of Villalobos, who after his night of prayer had told the priest he wished his help with the bell.

He found the carpenter working on the roof of the chapel. This morning, Villalobos explained, he wanted to try to fit the bell to the belfry—to test the strength of the supports as well as the sound of the bell. He had an abundance of help, he said, pointing to the large number of Spaniards and Indians waiting on the ground below. When they had raised the bell, he would ring it—gently, he promised the priest—to make certain it was properly suspended. He had had no experience with bells. Father Serra would have to advise him.

This was an important day for Manuel Villalobos, the priest thought fondly. For some reason nothing was so important to these men far from their homes as the familiar sound of the church bell. Villalobos was proud of his work and as eager as the other men to hear the sounds they had heard all their lives. Father Serra laughed to himself. He was as eager to hear the bell as any man on this shore. And while the men tugged and sweated, he watched and prayed that all would go well with the bell today, tomorrow, and on all the days when its sweet sounds would be heard down through the valley and out across the sea.

"Ring it!" one of the soldiers shouted when the bell had been fitted into the belfry frame. "Ring it!" he called to Villalobos who had not yet descended from the roof.

"May I ring the bell, Padre Junípero?" Villalobos asked.

The priest shook his head. "No," he said, "we must wait. Let those on the *San Antonio* be the first, as well as we, to hear the bell. They will have merited this pleasure, too."

He walked back to his own camp, sat down at his small table, and described in a letter to the Bishop of Mexico the progress made in the stockade as well as his problems of conversion. He had worked for nearly an hour on this letter, which with the others he had written would be carried back to Mexico upon the arrival of the *San Antonio*, when a small figure appeared in the doorway and called to him in a frightened whisper. He pushed his spectacles closer to his eyes to see who it was and then he recognized the girl whom he already called María.

On her face was the set, distorted look of terror—the look that takes possession of a face when the first wave of terror has passed. She stood in the doorway, her body fluid, almost in motion, ready for flight.

"What has happened, María?" the priest asked, getting up from his chair, and moving toward her.

The girl's dark eyes were fixed and brittle like the eyes of a doll, and her lips, dry and bloodless, parted to speak two words: "Boy . . . come."

The priest did not hesitate but followed the girl as she

ran toward the gate of the stockade. At the gate she stopped to wait for Father Serra and when he started to accompany her out of the stockade she shook her head frantically and forced two more words through her lips: "Mule . . . far."

By the time he had saddled his mule and had reached the base of the hill, she was lying on the ground, resting while she waited for him. As soon as she saw him she ran toward the forest and disappeared.

The forest seemed oddly unfamiliar to the priest on this sunless morning. A shapeless vapor hanging low over the ground kept him from seeing the trees that had been his landmarks, and the mule was forced to find the path almost without direction.

Unwarmed by the sun the air was thick and fetid, and the smell of rotting ferns and mosses spread over the path from the deeper woods. Now and then a gust of wind came charging down the path, sweeping away the suffocating mists and the forest stench, then disappearing overhead through the trees.

A deep rumble of sounds came out of the woods—the distant roar of wild animals blending with the shrill, staccato cries of invisible birds, the monotonous whining of mosquitoes, the blurred buzzing of swarms of bees, and the almost petulant whirring of clouds of gnats. The rumble was menacing, prophetic, but as he rode farther along the path and looked at the moving clouds above him the priest caught the significance. The wildlife around him was waiting for the rains that would put an end to the long summer drought. It thirsted for water and now that it smelled the coming moisture it was calling out for it with all its remaining forces.

Large, iridescent flies settled on the mule's rump, too lethargic to fly away but alive enough to sting and draw blood from the unhappy animal. Swarms of gnats shot around Father Serra's face and hands. Incredibly agile, they attacked him, leaving a drop of blood and a sharp, hot sting. They were too many to be brushed away and the priest settled down on his saddle and decided to endure them. Surely he would not have to ride much farther. By now he must be close to the village. In his anxiety, which had changed the space and texture of time, he felt that he had been riding all day.

Suddenly he saw overhead what at first he mistook for a strange formation of black clouds, and then recognized as swarms of hovering vultures waiting for that moment when a man or an animal—wounded or exhausted—is finally forced to yield. Horrified by the sight, he urged his mule on toward the spot that seemed to be the encircled area.

At that moment the girl appeared in the path and beckoned him to follow her. When he reached a small clearing less than a quarter mile from the path, the scavengers were circling directly above him.

The weary priest was prepared to find Francisco dead, but he was not prepared for what he found in the forest and he wondered that the vultures had not already descended upon it. The boy had been bound with long strips

of sailcloth to a dead tree which formed a clumsy cross
(the priest supposed this had been a grotesque accident)
and then he had been beaten until his enemies believed
him to be dead. Or perhaps his enemies had been frightened away, for one of them had dropped his blood-smeared
lash—the kind used by the Spaniards to beat their mules—
at the foot of the tree.

They had cut deep into his back with their whips, for it
lay open in great gashes; then they had bound his back to
the tree and beaten him again, for the front part of his
body also was hideously slashed into a crisscross pattern
of long, narrow red ribbons. His eyes were closed and his
mouth smeared with blood. His whole face had been
beaten, for he had been so bound that he could not protect
it with his hands. Strangely enough his hands had escaped
the lashing, and they looked almost obscene in their pale-
ness against the crimson of his body.

Who were they? Who had done this? The priest thought
immediately in terms of "they," for no single man had the
strength so to destroy a body without destroying his own
at the same time. But he lost no time in conjecture or even
in prayer. His first temptation had been to throw himself
upon his knees and beg God to reveal to him why men did
these things. Why, why, why? Was life so long that men
felt free to cut it off whenever and wherever they pleased?
Did they not die soon enough without wishing to destroy
each other? was hatred so sweet that men must prefer it
to love?

But even while he asked his God for an answer to these
questions he worked frantically to untie the strong knots

that held the body to the tree. Then the girl brought him a stone—sharp on one end as a knife—and with it he slashed at the sailcloth until the knots gave way. Gently, with the girl's help, he laid the body down on the thick moist grass, and then he stood up to wipe the sweat from his eyes with his shaking fingers. He had felt no life in the boy at all, yet his body was still warm. The vultures were flying in wider circles as if they hated the smell of life that now surrounded their prey.

The priest opened the waterbag that he always carried when he rode his mule, and kneeling again beside Francisco, he forced some of the warmish liquid through the boy's lips. Then he poured some of it on his handkerchief and wiped the blood from the boy's face. He leaned over his body to listen to his heartbeat and then put his fingers on Francisco's pulse. He felt a slow, faint pulsebeat like a far-off, almost inaudible drumbeat.

The girl watched, now looking at the priest, now at Francisco. Some of the terror had gone from her face, but her eyes were still staring—as if they had seen something they could never for a moment forget. Only her expression changed—and it changed rapidly from hate to anger to love and pity and then to hate again. The priest wished she could speak his language. He would like to know what passed through her mind.

"María," he said abruptly, rising to his feet. "I cannot carry Francisco to the camp on muleback. He would die. I must bring help. You must stay here with him." She nodded her head violently as he explained his words with gestures.

He pointed to the vultures that still hovered over the clearing. "You must not leave him for a minute. Do you understand?" Again she nodded her head and put her hand on the waterbag.

"Yes," the priest said, "give him water. Give him water and pray, María, pray."

She looked at him, confused by his strange words, and he explained, showing her by his example what she should do.

"Get down on your knees and pray, María—pray to God."

"God," she whispered.

"Say 'God, God, God.' Do not stop saying it until I return."

He climbed painfully back on his mule and smiled at the girl, but she was not watching him. She was kneeling beside the boy, and looking up at the vultures. Her lips were moving, forming the words "God, God, God." Like the boy's pulsebeat, the words sounded like a distant drumbeat in the ears of the priest as he hurried his mule along the path back to the camp.

*   *   *

In less than two hours the priest had returned to the clearing with the camp surgeon and four men to carry the litter. The boy and girl had vanished. Nor were the vultures to be seen.

"The Indians must have found them," Don Pedro the surgeon said. "It is just as well. We can go back to camp.

"I do not understand why the girl did not go for help in

the village in the first place," he continued with some petulance. He had been interrupted in the middle of a card game, and the trip to the forest had frightened him.

"The boy Francisco must have spoken to her. He has no faith in the shaman—and a great deal in the white men —despite his poor luck with them," the priest explained.

"He has faith in you, padre," the doctor said, "but what can we do?"

"I think it is best for you to return to the camp," the priest said. "I shall ride on to the village."

The doctor protested. "I do not think it is a wise thing to do, padre. The Indians cannot feel friendly toward the white man at this moment."

"No," the priest said, "they cannot feel friendly."

"Then . . .?"

"I go safely, Don Pedro."

This time the priest carried a bag of salt and the herb poultice, which he considered superior to any of the healing salves used by the camp surgeon. The poultice had been prepared by a veterinarian who had used it for injuries to the animals in his care. The priest had found it healing to the festering spot on his own leg.

When he reached the village he found it completely abandoned. The Indians had vanished with even their household equipment, and except for a few smoldering fires the village might not have been inhabited for many years.

He rode through the village to Francisco's house and into the walled enclosure. The sudden disappearance was significant. The Indians had not yet finished with the funeral rites for the Old Man of the Village and the girl Cecilia. Only a grave thing would drive them out of their homes at such a time. A grave thing like the death of their new chieftain.

He tied his mule to a tree near the big assembly house and walked down to the river. He would wait. He would wait here. Perhaps someone would come back to the village. He believed that the boy was still alive.

A man—a man like Francisco—could endure anything, everything. That, Father Serra told himself, was what was both splendid and pathetic about men. They were magnificent in their capacity for endurance. It was as if a man prepared a noose for himself, put his head into it, and then in some more than human manner saved himself from hanging. Nor could Father Serra console himself by believing that men would ever learn anything from past hangings or near-hangings. Generation after generation continued to prepare its nooses. . . . He thought about María. A girl like María would not have the strength to save herself or the man she loved from a noose. But she, María, would not have prepared the noose in the first place.

The priest then considered his own problem. All his work with the San Diego Indians had been destroyed. Not only had the white men and their God failed to move the Indians to Christianity, but they had driven them from the home they had occupied for an incalculable length of time. It would have been better, the priest forced himself to confess, if the white men had never sailed into this harbor. But he could not give it up. He could not give up the hope of conquering the soul of the boy Francisco, which could establish an invaluable pattern, for many would follow where Francisco chose to lead them. First, however, the body must be saved and then healed. Once more the limit of time challenged the priest. Two more days to heal a body and win a soul. He would not yield now—not even if he had to spend the night beside the river whose shallow water was scarcely able to form a sluggish mud in its basin.

Just before sunset he saw the girl again. She was approaching him from the house of the shaman. He got to his feet and walked toward her. As soon as she was certain he saw her, she turned back to the house and disappeared.

This time he found the boy living on a pile of rabbitskins on the bedroom floor. No one but the girl María was in the house. Life was more apparent in the boy now but he still seemed to be unconscious. The priest asked María to boil some water in the fireplace back of the house. Then he dropped some salt into the water and bathed the wounds with warm salt water. The boy shuddered but did not open his eyes. When he had finished with the salt-water bath, the priest covered the boy's whole body with the healing poultice. Then he sat down beside María and together they watched.

While he watched the priest wondered what had happened to the shaman and the other Indians, but he was too exhausted to question the girl with gestures. He supposed they were waiting—waiting for the young chieftain to live or to die. He wondered, too, about the boy's mother. Why had she, too, abandoned her son?

It was perhaps an hour later that the boy moved and opened his lips to speak.

"Father Serra," he said with more vitality than the priest would have believed possible, "you will please make me to live."

The Eighth Day

The Eighth Day

MORNING CAME but made itself evident only in the change from a deep, shadowless black to a weblike gray mist that hung in graceless garments around the houses and walls and trees. The rain was heavy in the clouds like a creature in a womb ready to be given birth, but the ground was wet only from the fog that formed a solid curtain outside the shaman's door.

During the night Father Serra had covered Francisco with his heavy cloak and the boy still lay motionless on the pile of rabbitskins. María, wide awake from love and anxiety, lay close against him as if in such a way the life in her own body might move miraculously into his.

The tired priest had fallen asleep several times during the night, waking with a start and a murmur of apology for his weakness. Each time María had smiled, then turned again to the Indian boy beside her.

Now in the reluctant light of the morning Father Serra looked down upon the two young figures so close to him: the helpless, beaten body of the boy; the tense, alert body of the girl who waited anxiously for some motion or sound that would indicate his return to consciousness. Once she touched his cheek with her dark fingers to feel the stirring

of life and seemed satisfied that at least he had not retreated farther from her.

So the first two people of a new and lonely world might
have lain together, the priest thought—the man asleep
from some enormous fatigue, the woman tender, watch-
ful, devoted. And these two were alone here—except for
the priest and the knowledge that on top of the hill were
white men, both good and evil, and that deeper in the forest or farther inland were brown-skinned men, good and
evil too, but of a goodness and a wickedness familiar to
them.

The goodness white men brought with them to foreign
lands had always more than balanced the sorrow that accompanied it, Father Serra believed with all his heart.
Why this failed to be true in San Diego he had not been
able to determine in the simplicity of his reasoning. In San
Diego he was unable to reaffirm his own philosophy, yet
never had he prayed with such intensity of body and soul.
During the night that had just ended he had prayed first
for the arrival of the ship, then for the recovery of the boy
chieftain, and finally for the strength to bring the white
men to a realization of the evil in them—its consequences
and its penalties. Then—finished with his prayers—he arrived at a course of action, a course of violent action, suitable, he forced himself to admit, to men who understood
nothing but violence. Since the comandante in his cruel indifference had refused to restrain his men, he, Father Serra,
would now make full use of the power given him, which
was the power of the Church of Rome.

Before he rode back to the stockade he showed María

how to prepare fresh atole for Francisco. The boy was breathing now without obvious pain. He had not suffered any broken bones, the priest was almost certain out of his long experience with illness, accident, and death. It seemed to him that this boy was suffering mainly from exhaustion and loss of blood. If his injuries were internal, he would live or die according to God's will. With a final look at the unconscious boy and a wordless promise to the girl that he would return, he climbed on his mule and rode back through the forest. Again he had no eyes for the forest. He saw only what he must do this day.

* * *

After the morning Mass, unattended by any of the gentiles, Father Serra went in search of the comandante, who was breakfasting in his own camp.

There was no doubt, Gaspar de Portolá told the priest, that Miguel Viamonte was responsible for the attempted murder of the young Indian chief. Viamonte, early that morning, had sent for three of his friends—the corporal among them—and he had undoubtedly planned the kidnaping and the attack.

"These men," he said, "are men of violent action. Here they are bored beyond endurance. They would do anything suggested to them by a man of superior force and intelligence. I am pleased, however, to hear from you, padre, that the boy is not dead."

"Why did you not put a stop to it, comandante?" the priest asked. "Your iron discipline has been celebrated in all parts of Mexico."

"To be quite honest, padre," the comandante explained, "I thought Viamonte had asked the men to come and play cards with him in the hospital—despite the early hour. When I saw them at midday with blood on their jackets, I told myself that they had gone hunting. Indeed they did return to the camp with some rabbits. It was not until I spoke with Viamonte after your departure that I feared some kind of disaster. The man was so quiet, so complacent. Had he been in a rage from the wounds inflicted upon him, I should have been more at ease in my mind. When you did not return to the camp last night, I was certain of the disaster. I sent six soldiers in search of you, and they reported a completely abandoned village. If I had not known that wherever you go you go safely, I should have sent every man in the camp to find you, Father Serra."

"I found only the boy and the girl, María," the priest said. "I have no idea where the rest of the village is concealing itself. But one thing is uppermost in my heart and mind now, comandante. This time Miguel Viamonte has gone too far. The Spaniards have never looked with horror upon the attempted seduction of a defenseless woman, but even they would not approve of the murder or attempted murder of an Indian chieftain."

"You are right, padre," the comandante said grimly. "Miguel Viamonte has gone too far. Attacking the head of a tribe, he has attacked the tribe. The Governor General of Mexico and the King of Spain will not be pleased."

"More important than that," the priest said hotly, "God is not pleased."

The comandante almost smiled. "I am responsible, of course," he said, "to the Governor General of Mexico."

"And I am responsible to God and the Church."

Gaspar de Portolá, who had been staring at his uneaten bowl of atole throughout his conversation with the priest, stood up and faced the small, angry man.

"What I mean to say is: my responsibility is more immediate. I shall put Viamonte and his friends in irons. They shall be taken aboard the ship this very hour."

The priest was silent for a moment. "You are filled with a feeling of virtue, are you not, Gaspar de Portolá? he said finally. "You believe that by imprisoning the body of Miguel Viamonte you make your peace with God, and—more important—with the Governor General of Mexico."

The officer looked at Father Serra in surprise.

"Why, what would you have me do—hang the fellow?" he asked.

The priest shook his head. "What you do with his body is no longer important to me. I am concerned with his relationship to the Church."

"What do you mean?"

"There is no place in the Church for a man without a soul."

"Then . . ."

"Then Miguel Viamonte must live . . . and someday die . . . outside the Church."

"You cannot be serious, padre."

"I am serious," the priest said sternly. "I, as of this day, shall recommend to the Bishop of Mexico that Miguel de Viamonte and his followers be excommunicated; that they shall no longer enjoy the privileges and the protection of the Church."

For a few minutes the comandante was too shocked to speak. He could only pace up and down the small space in his camp.

"You have given this careful thought, Father Serra?" he asked, suddenly sitting down at his table and pushing away the bowl of atole.

"I prayed about it all night, and my answer came from God. I am not discussing this with you, comandante. I am merely telling you what must be done. The Church is filled with men who give nothing to it, but only beg and accept. These men have to be tolerated. But men who menace the position of the Church must not be tolerated. They must be cast out. Miguel Viamonte has menaced the Church here as he has menaced it wherever he has gone. Through his actions—his accumulated actions, of which yesterday's was merely the conclusive one—the San Diego Indians are farther from God than they were before we came to this port."

"Yes, I suppose you are right," the officer said thoughtfully. "But you will first give him an opportunity to defend himself?"

"Of course. Before I prepare my letter to the bishop, he shall have this opportunity."

"Unfortunately I fear he has no defense." The comandante picked up some of his papers and looked at them. Shocked as he had been, he wanted to hear no more about the business of Viamonte.

"There is one more thing, comandante," the priest said quietly. "I hope you will bear with me a little longer."

"Of course." The comandante continued to turn over the sheets of paper on his table.

"I hope," the priest said, "I have endured with patience all the small humiliations you—and men like you—have constantly subjected me to. You have supplied me with the poorest equipment in the camp, and"—with these words he smiled a little—"the most miserable mule in your outfit. You have, from the moment we left Mexico, awarded me the least advantageous sites for camping. The space that was granted me for candles and incense and other materials customary for the worship of God you gave over to brandy for the diversion of your officers. When I, the representative of God and the Church, enter your camp, you remain sitting in the only chair. You do not offer me the smallest courtesy most Spanish gentlemen would offer any elderly man who came into their presence."

The comandante stumbled hastily to his feet, as the priest's words finally reached his ears and his brain.

"As I have said," the priest continued, "I bear these things patiently. Although I am human enough to observe them, I trust that I am sufficiently the servant of God to give them their rightful proportions. I forgive you these things, comandante. I bring them up only because I do not wish you to believe they have any relationship to the other thing I wish to say to you."

The comandante, flushed with embarrassment, was muttering unintelligible phrases.

The priest still spoke quietly, but a strange, metallic quality unfamiliar to the officer had come into his voice.

"My single wish," he said, "is to prevent the soil of New California from being made fertile by the shedding of blood. I have said this before. Now I demand it. You, Gaspar de Portolá, I hold personally responsible for every action of your men. If through your vicious disregard for human life one Indian is harmed, I shall recommend to the bishop that you as well as Miguel Viamonte shall live and die outside the Church."

Like many men who move through the world unmolested by any but physical forces, the comandante held in contempt a man whose spirit was that of humility, and although he knew in his heart that Junípero Serra was a man of unlimited power in the Catholic world—and his, the comandante's world—it had amused him to humiliate the priest. He had indeed laughed with the other officers when he had selected the wretched mule that was to be the padre's mount. It had pleased him to torment the priest and to allow him to stand while the officers sat. He had looked with contempt upon the priest's ragged, soiled garments, which contrasted violently with the well-brushed uniforms and polished boots of the officers. This was all true.

Yet Gaspar de Portolá was not an evil man or a weakling. He was evil only in his indifference to evil, weak mainly in his unselective attitude toward weakness. He was also a man to whom the thinking and feeling processes were painful. But now the priest had pushed him into a position where he must think. Listening to Father Serra he realized quickly that he must act according to the wishes of the priest. He would do this. He would command his men with care so that no destructive event would ruin his own life. Excommunication would surely ruin his life, and he did not for a moment question the priest's determination. It was his own good fortune that one more day would see the end of this miserable expedition in New California.

"I have a favor to ask of you, comandante," the priest was saying. "I am going to the chapel after I have spoken with Viamonte. I should like every Spaniard to stop what he is doing and come to me immediately. I have something to say to them."

The comandante moved hastily to the door, then stood back to allow the priest to walk out ahead of him.

The priest spoke briefly to the men in the chapel. He explained his reason for the severe penalty of excommunication and held up his hand for silence when a murmur of incredulity quivered through the crowd. Finally he told them that there was an element of danger in their position. The Indians had vanished either out of fear or to enlist the inland tribes in their defense against the invaders. He did not know which.

"Then if we are not to defend ourselves against them," one of the officers said, "why do we not abandon San Diego now—before the storm breaks?"

"You forget—we await the *San Antonio*."

"The *San Antonio* was wrecked long ago, Father Serra.

Why can you not persuade yourself of that?" the officer asked.

"Because it is not true," the priest replied. "The *San Antonio* brings the bells for the new missions, and no ship carrying church bells has ever been lost at sea. The *San Antonio* will come in time."

"But you mean in all seriousness," Manuel Villalobos said, "that if we are attacked by the Indians, we are not to defend ourselves? You ask a great deal of us, padre. To be killed by arrows that gunfire might stop."

"I do not ask a great deal of you. I ask you to be men, not killers of men. Perhaps this idea is new to you but it is not new to other men. I give it to you to think about and to remember, for to your children it will not be strange: To base the rights of a nation on superior strength is black tyranny. Its claim rests on the justice of its laws and on the fidelity with which it preaches the gospel to the ignorant. He who cannot understand this knows little of Christianity; and he who denies it is no more Christian than was Mohammed. Our only claim to this soil is through the Church. Yet look around you. You will not see the face of a single Indian who is here for the love of the true God. On the other hand, listen carefully and you will hear them coming. I hear them coming. Not now, perhaps not tomorrow, but I hear them coming by the thousands—in the years before us. Let no man among you raise his hand to stop them! And, if an attack should come, at least give your priest the first chance to defend you."

❈   ❈   ❈

Still the storm refused to break. The waves piled up frantically against the shore and twisted themselves around the rocks. The rain clouds hung heavy and menacing over the sea and land. The fog, so thick that the men could almost hold it in their hands, was pushed away, then back, and then away again by the winds. Through the fog the men could not distinguish one figure from another, and against the continuous, savage roar of the sea they could hear no sounds even inside the stockade.

Protected by the fog and the roar, the phantom figure of Tomás guided a wave of grayish figures over the wall behind the chapel. Then with all his strength the Indian heaved a lighted torch which missed the roof of the chapel and fell upon the top stone step in front of the chapel door. This was as far as his planning had taken him. Once inside the stockade he had supposed that luck and the confusion rising out of the fog would help the Indians capture the Spaniards' muskets. He had forgotten that he and his companions, too, would be confused by the fog. He hesitated, as a man not born a leader will always hesitate, waiting for the Spanish soldiers to run toward the firebrand.

But it was Father Serra who reached it first. Father Serra on his way to the sacristy with a supply of sweetmeats he had been hoarding for the fiesta was the first to see the firebrand and understand its meaning. He dropped the sack he was carrying, and hobbling up the steps of the chapel he seized the fast-burning torch and held it high above his head.

Still the only sounds above the sea were the shouts of Gaspar de Portolá, who was calling to his men, and the only visible figure was that of the priest standing beneath the light of the burning torch.

A soundless arrow passed the priest's head and quivered for a moment when it struck against the chapel door. Then followed the confused, rushing sound of men moving about, yet not knowing where they were going nor what they should do.

The priest moved down one step, and thrusting the torch in front of him he tried to distinguish the faces he knew were close to him. They were exactly alike. Covered with war paint they were identical, hideous, grinning masks. Even if his friend Tomás was among them, the priest could not identify him.

He stepped back and called out some of the names he had given the Indian converts at their baptism: "Tomás, Diego, Juan, Pedro, Sebastian, Pablo!" Still there were no sounds but the voices of Spaniards against the noise of the waves. The comandante moved within the light of the torch and again an arrow shot into the door, passing so near the priest's head that he felt its breath on his cheek.

Then Father Serra took another backward step and opened wide the door of the chapel.

"Come into the chapel!" he shouted, "every man in the stockade! Come into the chapel and get down on your knees and pray to the One True God!"

Another torch was thrown through the chapel door, This time one of Portolá's men rushed in to seize it.

The priest did not move. He called to the comandante.

"Bring your men in first," he urged. "The Indians will follow."

Gaspar de Portolá shouted an order to his men who ran to the chapel steps. Portolá was the first to reach the door. Father Serra stopped him.

"Leave your firearms outside," he said. "No man may enter the chapel armed against another man."

The comandante gave an order to the soldier nearest him, who ran to the cannoneers at their posts on the walls. Before he got back to the chapel the still-invisible cannons had been turned and were directed upon the Indians, who waited motionless for a command from Tomás, whom they had accepted as their leader in the absence of Francisco. The fog was breaking up.

With a willingness that would have astonished the priest if he had had time to give thought to it, the comandante and his soldiers dropped their muskets outside the chapel door and walked carelessly into the church. Under the benches were the loaded muskets the comandante had concealed there. The soldiers did not pick them up. They waited—as if for a church service to begin.

"Now," Tomás whispered to the men who surrounded him, "let us seize the muskets."

He ran up the steps and grabbed a musket, then motioned to his followers. In a few seconds they held the weapons in their hands and again awaited a command from Tomás. Still there was no move inside the church.

The Indian Tomás fumbled with the strange mechanism. Nothing happened. No evil-smelling smoke, no alarming sounds came out of it.

"It has no magic for us," he shouted, throwing it to the ground. "It serves only the white man. We shall have to burn the chapel. When the white men try to escape the fire, we must kill them with our own weapons."

At that moment a firebrand lighted up the wall at the side of the church and for a second Tomás looked through the dissipating fog and saw the face of a grinning soldier. And for the first time he noticed that the cannon had been turned upon the stockade. It had been turned upon the Indians—this monster which could destroy a ship, a whole village. The round, black evil eye was now fixed upon the Indians.

He understood now. The white men were safe inside the chapel. The evil black eye could not harm them. The magic had been removed from the muskets so that the Indians could not use them. The cannon had been made ready to destroy them the moment they tried to burn the chapel. Again a wave of fog concealed the cannon, but Tomás knew it was there—waiting. Again he hesitated. Boy-Whose-Feet-Are-Wings would know what to do—but he, Tomás, did not. He was not a leader. He wished he were back in the village with the women or in the forest with his animals. He should not have boasted to the shaman that he understood the magic of the white man's guns. Any man in the village would know better what to do at this moment.

Aware only that the Indians had stolen the muskets, which for some reason were of no use to them, Father Serra called out to Tomás in despair, for now he believed the white men to be completely defenseless.

Inside the chapel the comandante gave orders to his men. They were to wait for the sound of the cannon. They were not even to pick up the loaded muskets unless the cannon failed to frighten off the Indians.

But when the priest called out into the fog this time, a grotesque figure stepped out from the crowd and stood before him.

"Have you so quickly forgotten your God, Tomás?" the priest asked.

"We have not forgotten Him," Tomás answered. "He has taken no notice of us. We must avenge our chieftain in our own way."

"Vengeance belongs to God, not to man," the priest said sternly.

"Then let God avenge the chieftain now," Tomás replied. "Let God speak."

"God will speak." He called now to Manuel Villalobos, who hurried to his side.

"Ring the bells, Manuel," he said. "Let the Indians listen to the voice of God!"

At first Manuel pulled gently at the ropes that hung down from the belfry, so that the sound of the bell—sweet, soft, and clear—came to men's ears as from a great distance. Then it grew fuller and louder until it silenced the roar of the sea. A murmur of excitement trembled through the Indians, who began to crowd around the chapel steps.

"It is the voice of God speaking through the bell," the priest said to Tomás. "It has always been the voice of God. Tell this to the others."

The desire to fight and destroy—never strong in Tomás —had gone out of him. The other Indians still looked to him for leadership. And while he talked with them the priest called again to Manuel. "Louder, louder!" he said. "Let the whole world hear the voice of God!"

Manuel pulled with all his strength and the sound of the bell, angry now and commanding, shook the walls of the chapel.

The Indians no longer hesitated. One by one they dropped their bows and arrows on the steps and crowded into the chapel. The priest counted them as they entered and sighed with relief. These were the men of the village —and no more. They had not gone inland to enlist the aid of neighbor tribes.

*   *   *

Late in the night Father Serra remembered the sack of sweetmeats he had dropped in his haste to seize the firebrand from the chapel steps. He walked over to the chapel to recover it, for it was an important part of the fiesta he had planned for the following day.

On his way he passed the corral, and believing he heard voices whispering inside, he stopped. Surely the Indians were not attempting to steal the horses. But there was only one voice inside—one man. Tomás in all his hideous war paint was kneeling by the colt, talking softly into her ear— in Spanish. The priest hurried on to the chapel.

Inside the sacristy a small light was burning, and when he opened the door he saw the figures of two women. One held a torch while the other was busy with the utensils of the sacraments. The priest was speechless with horror. Then he recognized Francisco's mother and the older sister who bore the name of Marta and he saw what must have happened perhaps before the firebrand had been tossed against the chapel. The sacristy had been pillaged and now the two women were quietly but awkwardly going about its restoration.

Marta smoothed out as best she could the soiled, torn altarcloths and the rumpled vestments. With a piece of rabbit fur she polished the muddy vessels and the candelabrum and the precious gold-lined chalice. She was talking with the older woman while she worked and their voices, though soft, were angry. Women restored what men destroyed. It was this waste, the priest supposed, that angered the women.

His first impulse was to seize the holy vessels and send the women back to their homes. Then he reconsidered. He asked God to forgive the sacrilege and quietly shut the door and returned to his camp, completely forgetful of the errand that had taken him to the chapel. He kept remembering the woman's face, for when he had finally closed the sacristy door she was smoothing out the wrinkles in the garment of the beautiful image of the Son of God. It might have been the garment of her own son.

Another happy thought came to him. Francisco must still be alive. Otherwise his mother would surely not have come to help restore order in the sacristy.

❧   ❧   ❧

Two hours later the storm broke. The heavens seemed to burst into pieces as the lightning made great gashes in the black clouds, and the roar of the sea was feeble under the rushing rolls of thunder. At moments the sky was as bright as if the sun were shining and the silver sagebrush and yellow sea marigolds of the coastal hill glittered beneath the light.

When the clouds had ripped open, the rain began to fall—at first in gigantic bursts, then in solid sheets. In the stockade the men ran frantically in search of shelter, for the camp had not been built for protection against a storm like this. Finally they assembled in the hospital, for next to the chapel, which still lacked a part of its roof, this was the sturdiest building.

"What of the *San Antonio* now, Father Serra?" the comandante asked. "It cannot survive such a tempest, if, as you believe, it is near these waters."

"The storm will soon dissipate itself," the priest said. "Tomás tells me it is too early in the season for the regular rains."

For a moment he smiled. To the ears of a man like Gaspar de Portolá his own optimistic faith must sound childish, unreasoning, unmotivated. Yes, he thought to himself, such a faith must be offensive to the comandante, who believed only what he heard and saw with the ears and eyes of his body. Then he forgot about the officer completely. He spent the remainder of the night on his knees.

The Ninth Day

The Ninth Day

O N SUCH a morning the bright angel of Life and Light
might have rolled the stone away from the tomb
after the long black days of Sorrow. On such a morning,
Father Serra thought, St. Francis might have awakened in
the blue Italian hills and found himself blessed with the
stigmata of his Savior. Nature never exhausted herself;
whatever her travail, she always refreshed, always restored
herself, and the resurrection was inherent in her. The
clouds, free from their burden of rain, had vanished and
the wind had softened into a breeze that merely ruffled the
sea, and when the priest left the protection of the cliffs he
watched while the clear, sharp colors of a cloudless sun-
rise gradually covered the water and the sky.

The sea gulls, driven into the caves or far out to sea, had
flown back to their own yellow rocks. Now and then one
of them returning alone from beyond the breakers looked
to the priest like a swift-moving ship sailing toward the
harbor; each time the disappointment cut deep into his
spirit.

For nearly an hour he stood on the beach, staring at the
horizon—as if with his own eyes he might create a ship
and bring it safely into port. He rejoiced that the storm

was over. On this serene day the *San Antonio* could easily make its way into the harbor, and with no trouble the crew and Portolá's men could carry its contents to shore.

For a short time the priest diverted himself by examining these contents in his mind. Separated from man-made things one gives them a greater merit than they deserve, he told himself, yet he looked forward eagerly to the candles, the incense, the new altarcloth and sacred vessels. He thought of the things that would delight the Indians: seeds, tools, cooking utensils, steel knives and bone needles, strange foodstuffs and fabrics. When he remembered the letters that would come with the *San Antonio* his heart jumped a little. He hoped there would be many from the brothers in Mexico—long, closely written ones bringing news both vital and trivial, as well as fresh ideas and opinions he could ponder over, since such letters were his only substitutes for the books and companionship he missed sometimes to the point of despair. And he hoped for one more thing—the pair of spectacles he had asked Father Palou to send him, spectacles he would not have to press tightly against his eyes in order to see as far as a yard away.

However, he had no time to spend in happy anticipation. Resolutely he walked toward the hill, then stopped at the base and took a deep breath. He wished that a miracle would suddenly lift him to the top. Until that minute he had not realized how tired he was—how his body would rejoice over a long night of comforting sleep. Thinking of this, he did not believe it was possible for him to place one foot before the other. He was tired and he was an old man, yet the work that was his destiny had actually just begun. San Diego was only the beginning. Between this port and the elusive Monterey he would need to establish missions. And perhaps farther to the north when this had been accomplished. At that moment he realized he would never finish, never go home. He would work and die in New California. The life before him did not seem possible, for while he hesitated at the bottom of the hill he could think only of the immediate pleasure of going to sleep.

Chiding himself for his weakness, he started briskly up the path and in a moment his tired body was forgotten. The contents of the *San Antonio* were forgotten, too. This was the day of the fiesta. Today the last beam would be nailed to the roof of the chapel. Today the ship would arrive and the bell would sing its greeting.

Inside the stockade he met extraordinary activity. Every convert and many gentiles whose faces were strange to him waited for him in front of the chapel. The Spaniards were waiting for the morning Mass, too—all of them except Viamonte and his companions, who lay imprisoned on the ship in the harbor.

He conducted his morning service with some difficulty, for he was unable to hold the attention of the Indians. Instead of listening to him, every Indian had his eyes fixed on the church bell. On their faces were shifting expressions of interest and curiosity and awe—as each waited to hear the voice of God speak to him through the sweet and angry sounds they remembered from the night before. The Spaniards were restless, too, distracted by the anticipation of this day's event. The *San Antonio* might arrive or they might return to Mexico. Whichever it was—it would be a change from the terrible monotony of their days and nights here.

After the morning Mass, Father Serra explained the fiesta that would follow the completion of the chapel roof. The strongest among them would help Manuel, who in spite of the heavy rain had managed to keep the log beams dry. After that there would be no more work. There would be singing and games and food until the arrival of the ship. When the ship was sighted the cannon would be fired and the bell would ring in salutation. Everyone would go down to the coast to greet the incoming ship and then return to the chapel for prayers. When the ship had been unloaded the comandante would take charge of the distribution of the gifts to the Indians from Mexico.

The comandante listened to the priest's earnest, eager words. For a moment he, too, was almost convinced that before the sun set the *San Antonio* would sail into the harbor.

*   *   *

After the midday meal, Father Serra walked down the hill for his afternoon rest, but he was too alert to sleep. He could not keep his eyes from the horizon. Even with his eyes closed he saw the great white sails of the ship as it moved fast toward its destination.

During the afternoon, while the Spaniards under Portolá's orders moved the remaining provisions and all but the sleeping equipment to the ship in the harbor and the Indians amused themselves with their own somewhat solemn games, eating greedily of the strange foods the priest had hoarded for them, Father Serra walked three times to his place on the sands. From there he had promised himself he would watch the arrival of the ship.

A few minutes before the sun set he walked down for the fourth time. This was the hour, the minute he had prayed for. Whenever he saw the arrival of the ship in his own mind he had always seen it at this hour—not in the early morning or at midday but with the sun setting behind it on a cloudless day.

As soon as he reached the end of the path and stepped upon the sands, his body trembling with excitement, he looked out across the sea. It was smooth and empty. Not even a bird troubled his vision. Hardly knowing what he was doing, he walked up and down the sands and watched the waves closest to the shore. Each time they swept shoreward they increased the space between themselves and the rocks. The tide was running out.

He walked around the cliff and stood inside the cave for a few moments, hoping that when he came out the horizon would be changed. Sweat collected in the palms of his hands, but he did not notice it. A strange emotion passed through him in great shocking waves which he fought off, for he did not know what the emotion was. Again and again he closed his eyes, each time opening them upon a redder sea but still an empty one. Everything left his mind but the ship. He might have been alone in the world with God and the invisible ship. As the sea grew darker and the sun—round and red and sharp in its outline—moved closer to the horizon, the priest thrust his arms out toward the sea as if he could hold the sun in the sky with his own hands and with the same hands bring the ship into the port. God would not fail him, yet the minutes were following each other into that eternity which was the past, and so far . . . He would not finish the sentence even in his mind. . . . If God failed him, it was his own fault and his own failure, not God's. If the ship did not come, in some way his own faith had been inadequate. He had not been sufficiently single in his purpose. He had been distracted by other events that had seemed important to him. . . . Again he closed his eyes, and when he opened them the sky, like the sea, was empty and without sound.

He felt so alone in a vast, unpeopled universe that the sudden motion of people toward him shocked him into a kind of panic. He walked in circles on the dry sand, then looked toward the hill to find a reason for the boisterous sounds. People seemed to be flying toward him from all directions, and Manuel Villalobos, the first to reach him, had thrown his arms around the slight figure of the priest and had kissed him soundly on both cheeks almost before the padre recognized him.

"The ship, Padre Junípero!" he cried and the tears streamed down his mud-stained face. "The ship, look!" With one arm still around the priest's shoulders, he pointed seaward. "God has truly answered our prayers . . . your prayers!"

The priest looked at the horizon, then pressed his spectacles hard against his eyes and looked again. He could see nothing but the sea and the sky.

"I see no ship, Manuel," he said finally. "Are you making a jest?"

Manuel laughed and hugged the priest again. "Indeed, you have need of new spectacles, my beloved padre. The ship is moving toward us from the south side of the horizon."

While he spoke these words, crowds of Spaniards pushed toward Father Serra and embraced him and kissed his hands. The Spaniards, laughing and crying and cursing jovially, embraced the Indians standing in quiet, smiling wonder at the behavior of these strange white men who for days had been either taciturn or belligerent. It had to do with the second ship and the priest and the new God, they knew. They had seen the ship, and now every white man was on his knees in the sand while the padre offered their thanks to God. When Father Serra looked around him, it seemed as if everyone in the world had run from all its corners to salute the arriving ship.

Now Father Serra stared again across the waters but still he could not see the ship.

"Where is it now?" he asked Manuel.

"It moves with grace straight across the horizon like a fine white bird," Manuel replied. "It is still far to the south of us."

"Does it seem to move in our direction?" the priest asked.

"Not yet, but it will when it comes opposite the harbor," Manuel said, unable to take his eyes from the white speck far out on the sea.

A man might live for many years, the priest was thinking, and yet point back to this single moment and know it was the most splendid time he had ever lived or would ever live. He might experience magnificent hours and days and years, yet know in his heart that the splendor could not touch this particular moment while he stood on a darkening beach facing the Pacific and watched the answer to his prayers taking shape and body and motion. He wished the boy Francisco could have been here, too. Francisco, with his extraordinary imagination and sensibility, would have well understood the significance of this moment.

"What of the cannon, comandante?" he asked.

Gaspar de Portolá shook himself out of a dreamlike tension and answered.

"We have no dry powder. It will be a long time before we can fire the cannon."

Gaspar de Portolá had to believe his eyes because he had nothing but his sense organs to believe, but he could not free himself from his overwhelming astonishment that the old man had actually accomplished this thing. He had actually prayed the *San Antonio* out of God knows where into the harbor of San Diego. What a remarkable old man the shabby, dreary-looking figure was! Now he could have anything he wanted. When the governor general heard that Father Serra had achieved this thing almost single-handed, at the same time converting the whole San Diego tribe of Indians with no help from the Spaniards, he would be willing to give him New California—if he desired it. Yes, the old man would be a tremendous power in the rich, fertile land of New California. From here they would go northward, and with the ship and the padre's luck they would doubtless discover the port of Monterey. There might even be finer ports to the north of Monterey. There was certainly something up there that interested the Russians. But even the settlement of Monterey and other missions south of it would be no small thing in the reputation of Gaspar de Portolá. Quickly he revised in his mind his reports to the governor general. It had seemed advisable, he would write, to make secure the mission at San Diego before moving northward. This security had been accomplished simultaneously with the arrival of the *San Antonio*.

Awe and admiration struggled against the irritation Portolá always felt in the presence of Father Serra as he watched the priest now. It was difficult for him to reconcile the deep-lined face, the inward-looking eyes, with a life spent in constant outdoor hardship. It was difficult for him to reconcile the wise, intelligent face with actions that seemed—to the comandante—childlike and without reason.

Father Serra turned from the sea to Manuel's face, then back to the sea. The crowd was growing quiet, for the white sails on the horizon were moving almost imperceptibly.

"Now," the priest asked anxiously, "where is it, Manuel?"

"It has almost reached the point opposite us. Now it will turn a little and sail toward the harbor."

A few minutes later a murmur passed through the almost silent crowds.

"Where, where now?" the priest said.

"It has passed the point opposite us. It does not seem to be directing its course toward us."

"There must be some reason," the priest said. "The winds—current."

"Of course," Villalobos replied. "There is a reason."

Nothing was heard for a while but the deep breathing of the men. Then one by one cries of disappointment came from the crowds who waited on the beach.

"It moves on across the horizon," Manuel explained. "It makes no attempt to turn toward the port. I do not understand this."

"It is not the *San Antonio* at all," someone whispered.

"It is probably a British ship."

"A Russian vessel scouting the Southern Seas."

"Of course it is the *San Antonio*," the comandante said impatiently. "But the stupid captain has lost his course. He was probably caught in the storm and does not know. where he is. The fool! We shall probably never see him or the *San Antonio* again."

Although he waited until the horizon was lost in the darkness between the sky and the sea, Gaspar de Portolá was the first to abandon the waiting, disappointed groups of men. The officers and their men followed him. The arrival of the ship meant less to them than it did to the colonists, who cursed the ship bitterly when it finally disappeared over the northern edge of the horizon. Then one by one the colonists, too, walked up the hill to the camp, leaving only the priest, Manuel, and the confused groups of silent, watching Indians . . . It was almost midnight before the priest found himself alone.

Father Serra, the only man who had not seen the *San Antonio*, was now the only man who knew it would return. He understood his people's disappointment but he could not understand their prompt acceptance of the ship's loss. Again and again he had explained that God's ways are not always clearly discernible. But was it not enough that their prayers had been answered, the ship had been sighted, the expedition would continue?

It was not enough. Through the dark hours that followed midnight Father Serra, with ecstatic gratitude in his own heart, waited alone.

He did not know how much later it was that he noticed the approach of a strange, shadowed group of figures. The moon was no more than a sharp horn-shaped wound in the sky, shedding little light upon the priest's surroundings.

When the figures came nearer he saw that they were walking with great care as if they were afraid of something. No, they were carrying a large flat object. There were four of them. Five, including a smaller figure walking ahead of them. Then he recognized the smallest figure. It was María. Not until they came within a yard of him did he realize what they were carrying. Gently the four Indians deposited their burden on the sands in front of Father Serra.

With the tule they used for almost everything they made, they had improvised a litter. They had covered the litter with rabbitskins and on the rabbitskins lay their young chieftain. The Indians, whom the priest did not recognize, spoke to María, who nodded and whispered her reply. They stared for a moment at the priest and then disappeared behind the cliff.

The priest got down on his knees and looked at the boy's face. From the thin light of the moon he could see that his eyes were open and life was manifesting itself through them again.

"Yes, it is I, Francisco," the boy said. "It is not easy to recognize me, but I am Francisco." His voice, though still weak, was distinct. "Fortunately the men were not able to break my strong bones. Nor did they spill enough of my blood to make me die."

Father Serra turned to look at María, who, on her knees too, could not take her eyes away from the face of her beloved. This was the love, the priest told himself, that with the love of God had saved Francisco's life.

Then Francisco was speaking again. "I wished desperately to come here. Tonight I crawled from my bed to the door and down the road. While I rested there for a moment, María found me. In time I should have succeeded in coming here without help, but this was better. It was María who thought of the carrying-bed. She had seen one in the stockade. María—for a woman—is intelligent. Even I had not thought of the carrying-bed."

"Well, Francisco," the priest said, "I can see you are indeed much better. But you should not have left your home. In time I should have come to the village to see you."

The boy raised his head and spoke to María. He wished to sit up. She helped him move to a comfortable position with his head leaning against her shoulder. He breathed heavily from the exertion and then spoke again to the priest.

"It is good to be awake again by the sea," he said.

"You should have come this afternoon," the priest said. "You would have seen the ship."

Francisco shook his head. "I did not know this afternoon that I wished to come."

"Why did you come, Francisco?" the priest asked.

"For two reasons," the boy said. "We knew—María and I talked of this—you would be alone. We knew that the ship had come and vanished like an old sun and you would still be waiting for its return. María reminded me that you—old and tired and with your poor leg—had come to comfort me. So we are here with you. It is good."

"Yes, boy, it is good," the priest said.

"You do not ask me the other reason, but I will tell you. María and I have spoken of this, too. We wish to marry together in your church. We wish you to marry us."

"You know what you are saying, Francisco?" the priest asked. "You know that first you must be baptized into the

Church, confessing your belief in the One True God? You know this?"

"Yes."

"Why, boy, why?"

"It is simple. I wish to believe what you believe. I know that what you believe is true."

"Even though the ship I believed in is not in the harbor?"

"The ship does not matter," Francisco replied. "I believe what you believe because I have this love for you in my heart."

The priest leaned his head against the cliff and thought about the boy's words. God did not prove Himself through ships and corn meal and bags of salt, but through men. Perhaps he had erred in giving so much attention to the ship and its contents. Yet it had not been for himself that he yearned for the ship's arrival, but for the continuation of his service to God. Perhaps it was not God's will that white men should settle in the land that had always belonged to the brown men. . . . Then why had God sent the *San Antonio* within sight of the land?

In spite of his confusion, he felt a growing elation when he realized that now his work in San Diego was finished and that it was good. The boy Francisco would not only be a good chieftain, he would be the spiritual leader of his tribe. He had been persuaded not by the poisonous drink and the sound of the bell, nor even by the arrival of a ship with its promised gifts, but by his belief in God through love for a servant of God. This was the way it should be, but this had never happened to Father Serra before. Perhaps it would not happen again.

The feeling of exaltation spread tumultuously within him. His heart pounded hard against his ribs and pools of sweat collected in the palms of his hands.

With a sudden flash of understanding he knew that this was God's answer. This was God's complete fulfillment of the novena. Love, not just a ship, was God's answer to his long prayers. This boy, who in so short a time had become a man and in whose spirit lay the vast, invisible future of southern California, had found the love of God. The love of God was indeed the completion, the culmination of the novena. The sight of the ship had been merely a symbol. The ship would return in due time, but that was not the important thing.

Quickly the priest got to his feet and held his arms out wide toward the sea.

"May God be praised!" he cried out. "May God be praised!"

The boy, not understanding the priest's emotion, made a painful effort to rise, too.

"Padre, padre," the boy said with a passion the priest had never heard in Francisco, "the ship will surely return! It must return! I feel that I could swim out to the sea and bring it in with my own hands—if only it would sail this way again!"

"The ship." Father Serra spoke the words as if they were foreign to him, and then, forgetful of his leg and his tired body—even of the boy and girl who stared at him in wonder—he turned toward the path and swiftly climbed the hill. He almost ran across the dark stockade and up the steps into the chapel.

There he seized the ropes that hung down from the bell and pulled at them violently and with all the power in his thin arms until the sounds of the bell rose high above the washing of the waves, and he could hear nothing but the voice of God.

"Let all men hear!" he shouted. "Let all men listen to the call of the bell and know that God is and forever shall be! Let the sound of the bell be carried far across the land and far across the waters that God in his wisdom has created for men. Let every man who hears the bell know that God has answered the prayers of an unworthy servant!"

How long he tugged at the ropes he did not know, for, exhausted by the climb up the hill and the violent movements of his arms, he fell unconscious to the floor.

He did not know that men came running to the chapel from all parts of the stockade to see what had happened and to believe that the good priest had finally taken leave of his senses. He did not know that Manuel Villalobos had then picked him up and carried him to his camp as he might have carried a child.

The Following Days

The Following Days

FOUR DAYS later the *San Antonio* sailed into the harbor of San Diego, and it was Father Serra who first saw the white sails of the ship when Captain Juan Pérez directed her course well into the harbor waters of the port.

No one but Father Serra had stared continuously and expectantly at the horizon during those long four days and nights, for, although the reluctant comandante had agreed to wait a little longer because of the priest's impassioned pleadings and because he realized that by waiting a few more days he had nothing to lose and much to gain, he had no faith in the ship's return.

For many minutes the priest was certain it was not the *San Antonio* but another white-winged vision created by his imagination. He closed his eyes, then looked again. If it was a vision, it was growing larger and coming near the shore. When the ship was almost upon him, the realization of what it was shocked him into an immobility he could not shake off. He could only stand there and wait for the ship to announce herself.

The men on the hill heard the ship before they saw her. While she rode into the harbor waters her cannons fired a series of salvos, and the men, without even waiting to dress themselves—the entire camp had been deep in the fitful, dream-provoking sleep of the hot country at midday—raced out of the stockade to the brow of the hill.

There she was—white, graceful, arrogant—as if she were aware of her enormous importance in the lives of men and the history of a great continent. The Spaniards only knew that she was the most beautiful thing they had seen in their lives, and if she was symbolic of everything that lay behind them and before them, they did not think of this. They stood for a moment on the brow of the hill almost unable to see the ship for the tears streaming out of their eyes. Then they ran—ignoring the path and tearing through bushes and scrubby trees—to the shore line.

While the priest waited, without the will to move or speak, the two scattered groups of men—those from the hill and those who had already lowered themselves from the ship—ran to greet each other with shouts of affectionate welcome and lusty embraces. The Indians had appeared, too, all of them—as if out of the sands. This was a fine moment, the priest thought, yet it could have none of the sharp splendor of those few isolated moments four days ago—when he had not seen the ship at all. For him the *San Antonio* had arrived on the ninth day of his novena.

The explanation of the mysterious disappearance of the ship was reasonable enough. Captain Pérez, certain that the comandante's colonists were now well established at Monterey, had given no further thought to the San Diego settlement. He had kept his ship to its northern course, and he had sailed into a small port two hundred miles south of Monterey to bring a fresh supply of water aboard.

There he had learned from the Indians that no white men had ever been seen this far north. Still doubtful, he had lingered for a day, sending out scouting parties to find some trace of the Spaniards. Then, with considerable alarm at what he might find, he had returned to San Diego—four days after Father Serra's novena.

✵   ✵   ✵

Late in the night Father Serra, depressed and somewhat melancholy, made a final visit to his place of prayer by the sea. This mood was not unfamiliar to him. It invariably accompanied his departure from a place he loved and might not see again.

He had preached his farewell sermon to the Indians. How many of these he had preached! This one differed little from all the others except that with long hours of Francisco's help, he had translated it into the language of the San Diegueños, and for the first time had been able to speak directly to them all.

Then, with Tomás at his side to interpret his words, he had told them he must go away.

"My days have been too few among you," he had said, "but I shall never cease to pray that they have been of comfort and value to you. Keep my love for you in your memory and God's love for us all in your hearts. I shall keep my love for you in my own memory and my own heart. In times of grief I shall remember your sorrows and in times of joy I shall remember your laughter. What I have given you, you have in no lesser way given back to me."

Some of the gentiles had understood what the priest was saying to them through Tomás's awkward explanation, but others did not. Those who understood him had wept. After the benediction they had come to him in the courtyard, one after the other, to receive his embrace.

Father Serra had also looked after the temporal affairs of his new flock. He had left his tired, old mule to Francisco's care, and he had made certain that Tomás received not only the comandante's little horse but the long-promised pair of jewels for his nose. All the Spaniards in the stockade had helped him distribute the supplies and gifts brought by the *San Antonio* by carrying the heaviest loads to the Indian village.

Tomás, too excited to be of help to the newcomers, had approached one and then another Spaniard to ask his eager questions. Then because he could get no serious answers from them he had come back to get them from Father Serra.

"There is a strange animal, padre," he had said, "with small sharp knives at the side of her head. She must be a female animal, for I can see plainly that she is with child."

"Those animals with horns on their heads are cows, Tomás, and they are not with child," the priest had explained. "The large bag you see is filled with milk. By milking them men may obtain quantities of liquid which is a fine and nourishing drink."

"These cows—they will remain here?"

"The plan, I believe, is to leave some of them here and to carry the others to Monterey."

"I should like to have a cow, padre," Tomás had said.

"She is a fine beast if she can be trusted not to use her knives against me. I could ride upon her to the village and then have the good liquid to drink. She might even be better than a horse. Not better," he added hastily, "than the little horse the comandante has given me. But I do not know that I can make myself ride upon her."

"The little horse is not a pet, Tomás. She is to be used in your work, and the cow is not to be ridden—like a horse or mule. She must be left alone to eat plenty of grass. It is the grass and the quiet life that make the liquid. Besides, there are not yet enough cows. These must be left in the stockade so there will be milk for all. Later there will be many cows so that every man may have his own.

"You will see," the priest had continued, "that the animals the white man has tamed for his own use all have their particular place in man's life. There is the horse, which will carry him long distances, the mule, which is trained to carry heavy loads, the cow, which furnishes milk and meat, the sheep, which supplies wool from which garments are fashioned. Now look, Tomás," he said, pointing to a load of crates being carried from a raft to the high dry sands. "In those crates are chickens, which have a different use."

"What are chickens?" Tomás had asked.

"Chickens are birds that lay eggs every day. Eggs, like milk, are a nourishing food. Moreover, if the eggs are left alone and allowed to hatch beneath the body of a mother chicken, more chickens are born. In a short time there will be abundance of eggs which can be eaten as well as chickens, which are an excellent food."

"I have eaten birds and their eggs, too," Tomás said, "but it is not easy to obtain them."

"Chickens are tame and do not fly great distances," Father Serra had said. "They lay eggs each day, however, only if they are properly cared for."

"The white man has indeed made wonderful things," Tomás had said. His eyes, opened wide to all that was happening before them, could not move fast enough to see all the Indian wished to see.

"God has made all things on this earth for the service of man," the priest had said sharply, "and man has adapted them to his own use and to the glory of God."

Tomás had not heard Father Serra's words at all. He was watching a black cat with three or four half-grown kittens. Accustomed to the vicissitudes that had been heaped upon her since her first day at sea, the mother cat had stretched herself out with complete indifference to discomfort on top of a huge cask that was being pulled ashore from one of the Indians' tule rafts. The kittens, not yet indifferent to sea water, struggled to find protection against it by crawling under their mother's body. One after another she pushed them away with her front paw only to find them again thrusting their little heads beneath the long hair of her stomach.

"Those," Father Serra had explained, "are cats."

"And what is their use? Do they lay—?"

"No," Father Serra had said hastily, "they do not lay eggs nor do they yield milk for man's nourishment. They kill rats."

"Rats?"